1/29

THE CURSE OF
DUNBAR'S GOLD

THE CURSE OF DUNBAR'S GOLD

•

Johnny D. Boggs

AVALON BOOKS
THOMAS BOUREGY AND COMPANY, INC.
401 LAFAYETTE STREET
NEW YORK, NEW YORK 10003

PRINTED IN THE UNITED STATES OF AMERICA
ON ACID-FREE PAPER
BY HADDON CRAFTSMEN, BLOOMSBURG, PENNSYLVANIA

For Rachel and Matthew

Prologue

High in the Rocky Mountains of western Wyoming Territory is a moaning cave. Haunted, so say the Shoshone. It is avoided by the Crow, who refer to it as the Lair Which Weeps. The Cheyenne simply call it *havese*, or evil. A reasonable man could attribute the wail inside the mountain to the wind, but even the most hardened cynic would be hard-pressed to explain the mocking laughter these noble red men claim to hear—and Indians do not lie.

And what the locals call the curse of Dunbar's gold far outweighs the lure of a hidden fortune. . . .

—from *Yellow Gold & Red Death*
by L. A. Chapman
Beadle and Adams Twenty Cent Novels
July 11, 1878

1

Chapter One

Southe Pass City was dead.

It didn't come as a shock to Wesley Anderson. He had arrived just in time to see the town go bust in '72. The town boomed, however, the following year with Alec Dunbar's strike, but Wes Anderson didn't see any of the wealth, and Dunbar didn't live long enough to enjoy his.

Four years had passed since Anderson had seen South Pass City. Four long, miserable years spent in the "Big House Across the River," the massive structure of white and red stone on the Fort Sanders Reservation near Laramie. The Wyoming Territorial Prison. Now he was out, free—more or less—after serving four years of a life sentence. Paroled, he told himself, for good behavior. He laughed at that, mirthlessly, and walked down the rotting boardwalks and dusty, windswept streets.

He turned at Price Street by the county recorder's office, crossed Willow Creek, and stopped at Grant Street. Two horses were tethered in front of the Miners Exchange Saloon, but Anderson walked past it and stood in front of the Sweetwater County Jail.

Shutting his eyes, he could hear the voices of four years ago. *Hang 'im! Hang the murderin' kid!* He could see the faces of the bearded miners, holding their torches, and hear the planks creak from the deputy sheriff's boots as he stepped to face the horde of people, raised his shotgun slightly and pulled the trigger, sending a load of buckshot over the lynch party's heads as the black powder fizzled and sparkled in the night sky.

"You lookin' for the marshal?"

Wes opened his eyes. A buck-toothed, pockmarked man with thinning red hair and worn buckskins studied him.

"No," Anderson answered honestly. "Just looking around."

The man nodded and lit his pipe. "Good thing. Marshal's in Green River. Deputy's around, but don't know where." He nodded and walked into the saloon. Wesley thought about following him. He had a few dollars in his pockets and a shot of rye would hit the spot, but he paused with his hands on the batwing doors and looked back at the picket jail, the iron bars in the cell window, and decided the Miners Exchange was too close to bad memories and the law. So he walked back down Price Street to South Pass Avenue, turning at what used to be the Houghton & Cotter Store, ducking behind Smith's Store and walking into Fort Bourbon.

The saloon wasn't crowded, so Anderson went to the bar. Kegs of whiskey lined the back of the building, a stone wall they called "the cave." In the old days, South Pass residents had stored food, and whiskey, in the cave at all times, and during Indian scares, they'd lock women and children in the back—along with at least one man to protect, they'd joke, the whiskey.

Wes slapped a dollar on the makeshift bar and told the bartender, "Rye."

The man dusted off a shot glass and poured. Anderson killed the whiskey with one swallow and nodded for a refill. It was stupid to come back here, he thought. Nothing here but nightmares and death. Someone could recognize him—though he had filled out with muscle, and his face had darkened from four years of hard labor—and ship him back to Laramie. He probably would have left South Pass City then, if a man hadn't stumbled in at that moment, tossed a dusty leather pouch in front of the bartender and cut loose: "Yahoooo! I'm rich!"

Anderson's luck, Wes would later say.

The bartender smoothed his gray mustache and smiled, then reached for a dirty glass and bottle of cheap whiskey, watered down just enough to keep it from eating holes in customers' stomachs. "Horace Breckenridge," he said, "it's been awhile." He filled the shot glass, careful not to spill a drop, and corked the bottle.

Breckenridge downed the rotgut in an instant, suppressed a cough and tapped the glass on the bar. "Again," he said. "But I want the best in the house, Louie. I tell you I'm rich!"

Frowning, the bartender pointed to the sign hanging from a deer antler:

ASK FOR WHISKY OR BEER

NOT MONEY

NO CREDIT

"You know the rules, Horace," Louie said.

Anderson watched as Breckenridge fumbled with the drawstring a bit, then emptied yellow nuggets onto the bar. The bartender gaped and quickly brought out his scales. Probably enjoying himself more from the look on Louie's face than from the effect of the whiskey, Breckenridge said, "I want a bottle of the best stuff, not that pig swill, and a clean glass."

After measuring enough gold, Louie tightened the drawstring and handed the pouch to Breckenridge, carefully put his payment in a tobacco tin, and locked it in his money box underneath the bar. He produced a bottle labeled Genuine Kentucky Sour Mash and filled two clean glasses, one for himself. Breckenridge jerked a thumb at Anderson and told the bartender, "Give the young'un a shot too."

"Hit a strike?" Louie asked. He flinched when the miner gulped down the liquor. It was fine whiskey to be sipped, not swallowed like water on a hot day.

"Better," Breckenridge said absently. "Alec Dunbar's gold." He pointed to the initials burned into the pouch, but the letters could be A.D. or P.O. or anything else.

Louie frowned.

"Just found this one pouch but I is on to it, sure enough," Breckenridge said.

Louie's frown turned harder. "Hadn't you better be getting back to Cora?"

The miner snorted, pocketed the gold pouch, and picked up the bottle, leaving the empty glass on the bar. "Cora can take care of herself. She's a good, tough kid. My mule's resting in the livery, and I'll be joinin' him soon enough. I'll head back when I has a mind to. Right now, I feels like howlin' at the moon. I'm rich! Yahooo!"

The few patrons laughed as the dirty miner disappeared through the batwing doors and into the streets.

Anderson sipped the sour mash. "New in town?" the bartender asked.

"Passing through," Anderson answered.

The bartender stuck out a callused hand. "Name's Louie Chapman," he said, and before Wesley could think he had answered, "Wes Ander . . . son."

Chapman didn't seem to recognize the name, so Wesley breathed easier. "What was that miner talking about? That Dunbar's gold?" He asked, thickening his Texas accent on purpose, making it sound as friendly as the Reverend Johnston at the annual Presbyterian picnic in Jefferson ages ago.

"Oh, don't mind him none," Louie replied. "Said he had discovered a pouch of Dunbar's gold. Legend mostly, probably hogwash, about a hidden fortune up in the mountains. Lots of men been looking for it, but then there is the curse.''

''Curse?''

''The curse of Dunbar's gold. Every man who has been up there looking for the gold has died. Avalanches, cave-ins, freezing to death, drowned, broken necks or backs—you name it. That fortune is blood money, so a spirit watches over it, they say. Alec Dunbar was a good man, and outlaws stole his fortune and cut him down like a dog.'' Louie laughed. ''If you believe in that kind of stuff.''

Anderson motioned for the bartender to refill his glass, tossing a piece of silver in front of him. ''You believe him?''

Louie shook his head. ''You saw the pouch. Could have been A.D. for Alec Dunbar. Could have been anything. Breckenridge has been looking in those mountains for years, never found much of anything. Though that pouch means he did find something. But there ain't no hidden treasure.''

Wesley Anderson glanced outside before examining a poker table. Horace Breckenridge could wait, he decided, and asked to sit in.

It was dark now. Over the course of a few hours, Wes had increased his stake, but he hadn't been able to forget about Horace Breckenridge—or that pouch of gold.

''It's your bet,'' snapped the man opposite him, a surly miner with a beard as black as the ace of spades and a temperament to match. What money he hadn't lost at the poker table he had spent on drink. Anderson could only hope the miner's luck was better in the gold mines than at a card table.

Anderson glanced at his hand, then at the pot. It was draw poker and he had three tens, an ace, and a seven. The pot looked to be around twenty dollars and his bet was three dollars. But again he looked at the batwing doors. He shuffled his cards and thought. He had sat down at the poker table solely to make money, which he had—one hundred fifty dollars, maybe one-seventy-five. He could use the extra money, for nothing came cheap out here, and he was pretty sure he would win this hand the way his luck was going.

But the miner at the bar had mentioned Alec Dunbar's gold, and that hand was stronger.

"Gentlemen," Anderson said, "I fold, and I'm calling it a night."

He tossed his hand onto the deadwood, the common term for the discarded cards, removed his gray slouch hat, raked his winnings into it, and carefully placed it back on his head. "Thanks for the game," he said.

A few of the players returned his greeting politely, but as Anderson stood, the black-bearded miner—Wert he was called—said dryly: "Mister, you got a month's wages of mine there. You ain't leavin' this game till I get my money back."

The smile vanished on Anderson's face and he took a step back from the table. "Mister," Wesley said as his right hand dropped near the revolver on his hip, "I ain't got all winter."

Growling, the miner kicked his chair behind him as he stood and grabbed for the revolver in his waistband.

But Anderson's hand flashed, and suddenly the miner was staring down the long, black barrel of a Colt Navy .36, cocked and deadly. The miner, suddenly sober, eased his hand from his gun, which was still in his waistband, and steadied himself, swallowing.

The saloon had gone as quiet as a church. Anderson spoke softly, "Toss the gun in the spittoon." Wert obeyed. "Apologize." The man mumbled something. "I'm leaving," Wes said. "If you show your ugly face outside tonight, I'll blow it off."

The cold wind ripped through his cotton shirt and Anderson made a mental note to buy a coat in the morning. But first he would find Breckenridge. With luck the miner would be drunk by now and willing to talk. Anderson had waited a long time for this. Four years.

He looked up and down the street before heading for the livery, cutting through an alley and crossing the footbridge behind the old newspaper office.

An eerie quietness fell over the edge of town near the livery stable, and the cold night had a similar effect on Anderson. He knew he should be excited to be this close to one hundred thousand dollars in gold but instead he had a feeling of dread as he entered the livery stable. He couldn't explain it.

The barn was pitch-black and quiet. Anderson groped for a lantern along the wall, finally found one, and struck a lucifer on the butt of his revolver. A horse snorted as the light fell across it. Another whinnied. The dread overtook Anderson again, and he shifted the lantern to his left hand and drew his Colt with his right. He moved forward cautiously, uncertain what he would find, but hoping to see the miner drunk in a stall or somehow identify the man's mule.

Something glinted in an empty stall as the light passed over it and Anderson stopped, raised the lantern higher, and went back to the stall. It was the miner, Breckenridge, asleep in the stall, and Anderson smiled at his foolishness, holstered the revolver, and slowly approached the man.

But as he reached the edge of the stall, Anderson knew Breckenridge wasn't asleep. And he knew someone else believed the miner had found part of Dunbar's gold. Or maybe—a wild thought struck him like a fist—there was something to the curse.

Wes Anderson was no stranger to death; he had seen it many times. But even he had trouble holding down his whiskey as he looked at the poor miner. Breckenridge's face was bruised some—apparently, his killers had tried to beat the information out of him. And then, either after he had talked or because he wouldn't, someone had knifed him viciously. No, Anderson, thought. No *man* would ever use a knife like that.

Two deep breaths later, Anderson went through the dead man's pockets. Empty. That didn't surprise him, though. They even took his whiskey bottle. Now what?

Something sounded behind him, and Anderson panicked. The killers? Or worse yet, here he was, kneeling over the body of a dead miner, a miner who had been seen with a pouch of gold earlier that evening.

Anderson turned suddenly, grabbing for his Navy

Colt, and saw the figure standing over him. "Don't," the voice said, and Anderson knew he didn't stand a chance, knew that his luck had suddenly turned sour. It always did.

He let the Colt go and slowly raised his hands, eyes fixed on the rifle trained on him and the shiny tin badge pinned to the man's vest lapel.

Chapter Two

Morning sunlight cast striped shadows across Anderson's face. He blinked twice and came full awake, surprised to have been able to sleep at all. Swinging himself upright in his bunk, Anderson looked around. The jail hadn't changed in four years, still small and cramped, though a few more names had been carved into the picket walls with supper forks or rough-edged spoons. He had the jail to himself this morning. After pulling a gray wool blanket over his shoulders, he reached into his left boot.

The deputy marshal had taken his gun belt and revolver, naturally, pocketknife, matches, and money. But he had left the pennywhistle that Anderson kept wrapped in a bandanna. Anderson wiped it off, pressed it to his lips, and began playing "Lorena."

A gift from his sister, the whistle had traveled with Wesley Anderson from home in Jefferson, Texas, to the gold mines. It stayed in his war bag the whole time. But for the past four years, he had had nothing but time and came to master the musical instrument much as he had learned to master the Navy Colt before. ''The Yellow Rose of Texas,'' ''My Old Kentucky Home,'' ''Southern Soldier Boy,'' ''Old Dan Tucker.'' He could play just about anything and once put on a private concert for the warden at the Wyoming Territorial Prison. Music had been his solace. It had helped keep him alive for four years. Music . . . and the thought of that gold.

His mind carried him back to the damp territorial prison. He entered when he was twenty-five, to spend the next four years busting rock, harvesting potatoes, and recovering railroad ties from the Laramie River—and learning to play the pennywhistle by ear in his cell. Four years in prison because he had been convicted of helping a gang murder Alec Dunbar and his men and steal the Scot's fortune in gold. Four years in prison for a crime he did not commit.

He tried to convince himself that he wasn't bitter about the prison sentence. He just chalked it up to bad luck. *Anderson's luck.* Besides, in 1873 Anderson had been lucky the vigilantes didn't hang him, lucky that deputy sheriff had sent that lynch mob scurrying home. He would still be in prison if it hadn't been for another piece of luck. Six weeks earlier, he had fallen into the Laramie River while working on a detail, pulling those heavy ties ashore for the Union Pacific. The current swept him downstream for miles before he finally made it ashore, half-dead, vomiting what seemed like gallons of the muddy water on the bank.

Anderson had pulled himself up and started walking

back to the prison gang. He had traveled a half-mile before he came to his senses. Go back to the penitentiary? Serve the rest of his life behind bars for something he never did? Wes took off running east instead, stole clean clothes from behind a hotel in Cheyenne, and thought about lighting a shuck for Texas, back home. Only he picked up a copy of the *Cheyenne Daily Leader* on a bench in front of a barbershop and saw the little headline on Page 3: "Prison News!" And the brief paragraph:

Wesley Anderson, convicted in the brutal slaying of Alec Dunbar four years ago, was swept down the Laramie River on the 12th inst. and is presumed drowned. The prisoner, one of the first to enter our new penitentiary, was helping recover ties for the Union Pacific Railroad, the warden reports.

They thought he was dead. Wes was free, but he had wasted four years of his life. Dunbar's gold weighed heavily on his mind. Four years in that rat hole, cutting ice from the river during the winter, breaking rocks in the summer, making brooms, working the river when he couldn't swim, playing foolish concerts for that self-righteous warden. He had a right to Dunbar's gold. The dead Scotsman had no family. The gold was there for the taking, curse or no curse.

Anderson's brown hair was long and shaggy now. He hadn't been to a barber since his escape, and he still wore the black corduroy trousers and blue shirt he had purloined in Cheyenne before drifting west toward the South Pass district. He quickly tallied all that he owned: stolen clothes, old boots and hat, plus a pocketknife and cheap watch he had won in a card game in Atlantic City, poker winnings from Fort Bourbon, a pennywhistle more than a dozen years old, and his Navy Colt and gun belt. He had worked for the revolver, breaking ten horses for a rancher near Medicine Bow in four days. The rancher even gave him the hat plus his pick of horse, saddle, and bridle—and a ten-dollar gold piece to boot.

"It's called a stake," the rancher told him.

"I . . . I . . ."

"You're a good lad," the man said. "Hard worker for sure, and I can tell you're an honest man. You'll pay me back when you get settled. I'll be here. Besides, I'll make a tidy profit selling them horses you gentled. Take it all, Mr. Smith, and good luck."

Wes Anderson promised himself that if he found Dunbar's gold, he would pay back that rancher—with interest.

As he finished the last notes of "Lorena," he heard the clanking of keys and saw the jail door swing open. The deputy, still dressed in a tailor-made broadcloth suit and holding a nickel-plated rimfire Henry rifle, leaned against the log wall and listened.

"Pretty," he said.

Anderson tapped the pennywhistle on his pant leg and put it on his bunk. "Thanks."

Neither spoke for two or three minutes. Finally the deputy said, "We'll see about getting you some breakfast, if you answer some questions." The words rolled out slowly in a rich Southern accent. Mississippi,

Anderson guessed, and from the look of him, a rich river town like Natchez or Vicksburg.

South Pass City, Wyoming Territory, seemed an eternity from those cotton plantations, beautiful belles, and muscadine wine.

Anderson didn't respond. The man was tall, he noticed, better than six feet, and was wearing a shoulder holster underneath his coat. His black boots were polished to a gleaming shine, as was his badge. He had sky blue eyes and blond hair, was clean shaven, and carried himself with confidence. Anderson had no doubt the man could handle that Henry rifle.

"My name is Paul Livingston. I'm deputy marshal. The miner was Horace Breckenridge. You were seen in Fort Bourbon. You talked to the bartender about the miner, you were at the bar when Horace spilled his gold nuggets. You almost gunned down another drunk miner. This being Sweetwater County, that's probably enough for you to dance at the end of a rope no matter how well you play that flute."

"Pennywhistle," Anderson corrected.

Livingston smiled. "It'll still hang you."

Anderson sighed. "He was dead when I found him."

"So what did you want with him?"

More silence. Anderson once beat a hangman's noose through luck but he didn't know how much he should reveal—especially to a lawman. But then the deputy, by the way he was dressed, seemed to be a man who enjoyed the things money could buy. And one hundred thousand dollars split two ways was still a lot of money.

"He was after Alec Dunbar's gold," Anderson finally said. "So am I."

The deputy snorted. "So are a lot of people. And many have died looking for it. What do you know about Dunbar's gold?"

Anderson was looking out the barred window again. He thought a minute, looked Livingston in the eye, and said,

"I served four years in prison because folks thought I helped steal it."

Outlaws ruled the roads from the Montana gold fields in the 1860s. Alec Dunbar had learned his lesson up north. He knew that anyone trying to move a fortune via stagecoach or wagon train with anything less than heavily armed guards risked losing his gold and his life.

The aging Scotsman, who had made fortunes in California during the forties, moved to the high Rocky Mountains in 1863 to make even more. He never hit it rich in Montana, and left Bannack City in the early seventies for the South Pass Mining District of Wyoming Territory. There, when most miners thought the hills had played out, Dunbar found the mother lode: one hundred thousand dollars in gold. He decided to bring it to the railroad in Green River, renting a hearse and hiring a dozen armed riders.

His only mistake was in the guards he had hired. Four of them actually rode for Major Jonathan Vaughn MacDermott, Connecticut native, Confederate deserter, gentleman, and murderer. MacDermott's marauders had been the scourge of western Montana

Johnny D. Boggs

years earlier before drifting south, robbing miners in South Pass and nearby Atlantic City. Dunbar and his men were ambushed on the road to Green River, barely out of South Pass. Dunbar himself was killed, as were all of his men, and MacDermott and his bandits made off in the hearse toward their hideout in the mountains.

"And where do you fit in?" Livingston asked after Anderson had finished.

"I had been mining, cleaning the livery, anything I could for months here," Anderson replied. "Then I rode out to see about working for Dunbar. My horse broke a leg in a gopher hole, and I just happened to hook up with Dunbar on his way from the mine. He took me in, though I don't know why."

Anderson laughed without humor. "Then Mac-Dermott's men hit. I took a slug in the shoulder and was left for dead. When the posse found me, they didn't believe my story—and I can't blame them for that. They thought I was one of MacDermott's men. So off to prison I went."

"Lucky for you," Livingston said. "Back then vigilantes were prone to lynchings or just shooting suspects on the spot. Wait a minute!" He left the room and returned in less than a minute, waving a newspaper.

"Wesley Anderson!" Livingston shouted. "Drowned in the Laramie River on a prison detail from the 'Big House.' You're Anderson?"

"I am."

Livingston shook his head. "You're handy with a

six-shooter, I'm told, and I don't think you picked that up in prison.''

''I was handy with it then. That's one of the reasons Alec Dunbar took me on.''

The deputy laughed. ''I had forgotten all about the marauder who got sent to prison. I could hang you. Or send you back to the state penitentiary for life. You have a preference?''

Anderson shrugged, playing it cool, though he was bluffing. Inside his stomach churned at the prospect of returning to prison—again when he was innocent—or, more likely, swinging from the gallows.

''What do you know about Dunbar's gold?'' Wes asked.

''Too many stories have been told by now to figure out what's real and what's made up,'' the Southerner said. ''Even saw a half-dime novel about it in the general store two years back.''

Anderson smiled. ''I read it in the 'Big House.' The author didn't mention me.''

Livingston laughed, then continued his story. ''There was a double-cross after the holdup. Vaughn MacDermott had a partner, Lee Thorn, who was off his rocker. After you got shot, they rode away with the hearse full of gold—and Alec Dunbar—and killed Dunbar. Then MacDermott had his men shoot Thorn, only Thorn was tougher than the others, killed a few, then took all of the gold and vanished in the mountains. People guess he buried it, then died. And no one knows where he hid the fortune.''

''I picked most of that up in prison.''

''MacDermott and his marauders disappeared

shortly after that. Vigilantes were getting a mite tired of the outlaw situation, as well you know. But people have still been going into the mountains, hunting for that gold. They say that Dunbar put a curse on it before he was murdered. Did you hear that in prison?''

Anderson nodded. ''And from the bartender and others. And that half-dime novel.''

''Well, I've been in Wyoming long enough to see dead fortune hunters brought in from the high country,'' Livingston said. ''And I've heard enough stories about others who went after that treasure and never came back. I reckon the talk of Dunbar's gold had been pretty much dead for the past year, until last night. Those stories finally scared most of the fortune hunters away. Even the Indians say part of those mountains are haunted.''

''Do you believe in ghosts?'' Anderson asked.

Livingston's eyes gleamed. ''Not really. But I believe in gold. You really think that miner found Dunbar's fortune.''

Anderson was silent for a while, letting the deputy stew anxiously. ''Well?'' Livingston snapped impatiently. ''Do you?''

''Alec Dunbar's hearse was full of strongboxes,'' Anderson said, brushing his long locks from his eyes. ''He showed me one pouch when he hired me, saying there was a pouch for each guard if we made it to Green River. Each leather pouch had 'A.D.' burned into it.'' He paused again before adding, ''Just like the one that miner had at Fort Bourbon last night.''

Both men thought silently for a minute, mentally comparing their notes. Their eyes locked, sizing each other up, this well-dressed lawman and a shaggy-haired young convict. And without speaking they knew they were partners.

Livingston reached into his trousers pocket and withdrew Anderson's pocketknife. "Breckenridge wasn't murdered with this, and I couldn't find anything in the livery that did the dirty trick."

"You letting me go?"

"Just far enough to get your horse, a coat, and some supplies. Meet me at the livery ready to ride. That sound fair, partner?"

Anderson nodded as he stood. "Where are you going?"

"To tender my resignation."

An hour later, with a heavy Mackinaw coat, plenty of powder and shot, and his pennywhistle, Wesley Anderson arrived at the livery, surprised to find Livingston waiting by a big roan horse and a mule loaded with mining tools and supplies.

"The mule was Breckenridge's," Livingston said, "and we'd better hit his place first."

"Think he left a map or something?"

Livingston shook his head. "Whoever killed the old man will be heading there with a half day's start, maybe more. I'm worried about Cora."

Anderson began saddling his chestnut gelding. "Who's Cora?" he asked.

"Breckenridge's daughter."

Chapter Three

Twenty-three-year-old Cora Breckenridge stopped at her mother's grave on the hill overlooking the rough-hewn log cabin she had called home as far back as she could remember. She eased the bucket of water to the ground and looked at the small wooden plank that served as a headstone. The words her father had carved had faded over the years, but Cora knew them by heart:

> ILEN BREKNRIGE
> Gon 2 GOD 1868
> ILL miss yee

Her father had promised to have a marble tombstone made up whenever he struck it rich, correct the spelling, maybe even carve an angel on it. But Cora preferred this weathered piece of pine. She could barely remember her mother, Eileen, but the image of her father painstakingly carving the marker, sobbing like a child with his wife dead of pneumonia, remained permanently locked in her mind.

The big dun horse in the corral snickered, and a mule snorted. Cora looked up, spotted the dust rising in the distance, and hurried toward the cabin with the water bucket. Alone, at the foot of the mountains, she had learned never to trust strangers, whether Indians, trappers, or townsmen. And with her father almost constantly gone, she was quite adept at taking care of herself. She took the double-barreled shotgun from above the mantel and leaned it against the wall near the door.

It was almost noon. Too early for her father; he never arrived until dusk or later, whether he was coming from the mountains or South Pass City. And she seldom had visitors, especially now that the mining district had played out and people were moving away. She squinted until she could make out the riders. Three of them riding hard. She walked to her father's room and found his boot pistol, checked the percussion cap, and stuck the single-shot weapon in her apron.

Then she stepped outside, staying close to the doorway and her shotgun.

Louie Chapman poured himself a shot of Kentucky bourbon and sipped it for breakfast. He pulled on the ends of his mustache and studied the dark, empty Fort Bourbon. The late Horace Breckenridge and his dirty pouch of gold gnawed on his gut like a starving coyote. A miner showing off gold in a saloon, then winding up stuck like a fat hog wasn't uncommon in a place like South Pass, though the Rocky Mountain gold towns were becoming more civilized.

But Louie had seen Deputy Marshal Paul Livingston and that young stranger ride out of town not a half hour ago leading Breckenridge's pack mule. Louie thought about that, and what it meant. And he remembered the stranger with the quick gun asking about the miner and Dunbar's gold. He remembered that pouch with the letters burned in the hide. He didn't care about the legendary curse—curses were for schoolgirls. What he cared about was that he was fifty-two years old and peddling cheap whiskey to foul-smelling, foul-mouthed miners and rogues. South Pass City was bust, and soon he'd have to pack up and start over at some other disgusting mining camp. He drained his drink in an instant, not caring that it was sipping whiskey.

If Breckenridge had found Alec Dunbar's gold, that would explain a lot. He could trail the two riders to the miner's cabin, ambush them and take the gold for himself, maybe move to San Francisco. But he would need help—and quickly.

Finding gunmen would be easy in South Pass though. And Louie Chapman knew where to start. He walked out of the saloon toward the Dutchman's Cafe, where he expected to find that grouch of a miner, Wert Pierce.

Paul Livingston poured Wes Anderson a cup of coffee as they rested their horses. Neither really had wanted to stop, but both admitted that it would be foolish to wear out their mounts, and they had ridden hard since morning.

Anderson leaned against a boulder and sipped the bitter liquid. It was too hot, so he set the cup by his feet and drew his Navy Colt, checking the loads and mechanism, enjoying the metallic clicks as he rotated the cylinder.

"I'm interested," Livingston said, "in how a boy leaves Texas, from your accent, and makes his way this far north."

Satisfied, Anderson holstered the revolver and picked up his cup. "My mother's wish," he said softly. Livingston's face was blank, uncomprehending. "My father had died at Shiloh. My only brother fell at someplace in Maryland, both wearing the gray. My mother gave me a Navy Colt and a Bible and told me to get as far away from the war as I could. My sister gave me the pennywhistle.

"I was fifteen in '63. Conscription was the law, though I was too young to be drafted, but younger boys had been called to fight. I walked to Fort Worth, freighted my way to Sante Fe, kept moving north."

Livingston nodded at the revolver. "You still prefer that old cap-and-ball antique. Seems like you'd go for one of the newer models that are easier to load."

Anderson shook his head. "The Navy fits my hand, and I'm used to it. As bad as Anderson's luck is, if I tried some new revolver, it'd blow up in my face."

"Well, I'm interested in learning what happened to the Bible."

A heavy sigh followed the sound of Anderson's cup

emptying the dregs. "Traded it for powder and lead."
Then he said, "I place you from Mississippi."

"You are indeed correct."

"Natchez or Vicksburg?"

"I am even more impressed. Vicksburg. I loathe
Natchez."

"So how does a Southern gentleman get from the
Mississippi River to western Wyoming Territory?"

Livingston kicked out the fire and poured the rest
of the coffee onto the coals, which sizzled. "The Yankee siege," he finally said, his voice bitter. "De-
stroyed my home. Everything. I was eating rats by the
end, living in a cave like some animal." His face was
inflamed, and Anderson regretted bringing up the subject. Livingston took a deep breath and exhaled. He
regained his composure and continued quietly.

"So after Pemberton's surrender, I was happy to
leave the Mississippi. I've drifted through Wyoming
and Montana for a dozen years now."

It seemed a good idea to change the subject. "How
far to Breckenridge's?" Anderson asked.

Looking toward the hazy, distant purple mountains,
Livingston guessed, "If we ride hard, maybe by
dusk."

Anderson stood. "Let's ride."

The three riders eased into a trot when they neared
the Breckenridge claim, then slowed to a walk. From
the look of their horses, Cora knew they had ridden
long and hard, probably from South Pass or Atlantic
City. They noticed her and headed for the water
trough, and one swung from his winded mount.

He was dressed like a gentleman, Cora thought, but a gentleman doesn't dismount at a person's home without being asked.

"Ma'am," he said softly, "I take it you are Miss Cora Breckenridge." His accent was impossible to place, bland, but his outfit was sharp. He wore fine gray wool trousers with matching vest, high black boots, royal blue shirt and a black silk cravat, loosened during the long ride. A red wool sash was wrapped around his waist, knotted on the left side with the tassels hanging to his knees, and he carried a brace of Colt's cartridge-firing revolvers, their walnut butts sticking forward.

Blond, clean-shaven, blue-eyed, handsome, though somewhat pudgy, probably in his mid-thirties, he could have been anybody: banker, gambler, lawman, or outlaw.

But his companions, still mounted, were trash. Dirty, unshaven, and slim, with little regard for their appearance or their horses. Even their saddles were worn and dirty; and her father had told her if a man couldn't keep his saddle clean he was worthless. Plain and simple.

The man removed a black Stetson from his head and stated, "I am John Mousiness from Atlantic City. And I fear I bring bad news."

That grabbed Cora's attention and she swallowed hard, knowing it had to be about her father. She looked into the man's soothing eyes and sputtered out, "My pa?"

Mousiness frowned and turned to his men: "Mr. White, Mr. Black, please wait outside while I talk to

Miss Breckenridge.'' He slowly approached her, put his right hand on her shoulder, and said, ''I'm afraid so. Let's go inside.''

''How come they didn't hang you?'' Livingston asked as they slowed their horses to climb a bluff. ''Or shoot you? Four years ago, most mining camps still believed in summary justice. *Justice*.'' He spit out the word like bad water.

Anderson took a sip of water from his canteen, shrugging. ''Just luck, I guess.'' He thought a minute, then continued. ''They took me back to the jail thinking I might lead them to MacDermott's hideout, at least tell them where it was. I stuck to my story. *My true story*. A deputy sheriff ran off a lynch party one night. A lot of folks wanted me dead, but the judge and jury took mercy on me.''

''Life in a territorial dungeon, especially if you're not guilty, doesn't sound too merciful to me.''

''You sound like you're talking from experience,'' Anderson said, putting the canteen back on the saddle horn and staring at Livingston, trying to read his new partner. But Livingston only smiled and changed course.

''Yes, the law was taking hold by then, just as it had in Bannack, Virginia City, Nevada City, all of the Montana camps in the sixties. They finally got tired of all the outlaw gangs. Hanged most of them, killed their share, ran the rest out of the territory.''

''Including MacDermott.''

Livingston didn't know whether Anderson had meant it as a statement or a question. He nodded.

"Vaughn was last seen in these parts for sure back in '75. You hear rumors, though. Deadwood. Denver. Dodge City. Even Texas. And every once in a while some nearby mining camp. Who knows where he really is? Even if he's still alive."

Cora had promised herself that she wouldn't cry, but here she was bawling like a newborn calf on this stranger's shoulder. She hated herself for it, but she couldn't stop.

"Why?" she finally asked. "Why would anyone want to kill Pa?"

The man called Mousiness eased her into a hand-made chair near the table, before sitting down himself. "I fear it was robbery," he said, withdrawing an empty leather pouch from his vest pocket. "Did you ever see this?"

She stared at it briefly and shook her head.

"It contained gold," the man said. "He was seen buying a bottle at a South Pass saloon. He said he found part of Dunbar's gold. Does that mean anything to you?"

Cora sniffed and she wiped her green eyes with a bandanna Mousiness had given her earlier. "He was always looking for it, or something. I warned him about the curse though, and now, now . . ." She was crying hard again and Mousiness sighed.

"Dear," he said softly, "the curse is superstition. Your father was murdered by a man. Where was he camped last? Do you know?"

She shook her head rapidly. "Somewhere up north, toward the Yellowstone. I seldom went with him."

She stopped suddenly, remembering. "But," she began.

"Yes," Mousiness said anxiously.

"Before he left last, he said he would be trying near Gunsight Pass."

Mousiness stood. "I'm not familiar with that."

"It's just what we called it; it isn't on the map. It's on the Divide, a little pass that we thought looked like the gunsight on a rifle."

Mousiness knelt by her, grabbed her hands, and looked at her pleadingly. "Cora, could you help us find this pass?"

"Major MacDermott," a raspy voice called from the doorway. "Lane and me is tired of waitin' outside."

The man called Mousiness rose angrily and turned to the tall, leathery man leaning against the door frame. "Keno, you fool. Get outside!" Then he turned back to Cora, the kindness gone from his face, his eyes burning in anger as recognition came to Cora.

"You!" she said. "You're Vaughn MacDermott, the assassin and thief. *You killed my pa!*"

Cora was on her feet in an instant, reaching for the single-shot pistol in her apron, but MacDermott grabbed her shoulder with his left hand, gripping it like a vise, and powerfully slammed her back into her chair as the man in the doorway, Keno, laughed hollowly. MacDermott ripped the boot pistol from her apron and threw it across the room.

"All right, gal," MacDermott said. "You're taking us to Gunsight Pass, helping us find that gold, or I'm turning you over to Keno and Lane Morris. And when they're through with you, even a buzzard wouldn't touch you.''

Cora answered by spitting in the outlaw's face.

Seething, Vaughn MacDermott, Connecticut native, Confederate deserter, gentleman and murderer, savagely slapped Cora's face.

Chapter Four

Darkness was approaching rapidly when Anderson and Livingston arrived at the Breckenridge claim. Sensing danger, the two eased their way toward the cabin, Livingston holding his Henry rifle and Anderson his Colt.

Anderson swung from his chestnut and entered the cabin through the open door. An overturned chair and stained blood on the dirt floor caught his attention. He swore quietly, worrying over a girl he had never met. A vision of the brutally knifed body of Horace Breckenridge flashed before him, and he knew he had reason to be concerned about the girl's safety. There was little blood on the floor, though, and he guessed that she— or whoever had been in the cabin—had either a busted lip or nose. He stood, went through the small cabin, found nothing, and walked outside.

"Her horse and another pack mule are gone," Livingston said. "And somebody went through the old man's shed looking for something. Looks like they took some extra shovels, picks, stuff Breckenridge had.'' He added hopefully, ''Maybe she left before they got here.''

Shaking his head, Anderson told Livingston about the dried blood and overturned chair. He studied the ground near the cabin in the dim light. ''Three horses rode in,'' Anderson said. ''We know that. But I count five sets of tracks, including the mule's, heading out.

''Three pairs of bootprints lead into the cabin. Those and a small set of prints came out.'' Anderson had dropped to a knee as he fingered the tracks, moving forward slowly toward the corral. ''Small set is in front, looks like she was pushed.'' He pressed his finger to a brown spot in the dirt. ''More blood, but not much.''

Anderson studied the signs a few minutes more before walking back to Livingston. ''My guess is that they tied her up, forced her on her horse, and rode out.'' He pointed to the mountain range. ''They've got her,'' he added. ''And they've already killed at least once.''

Paul Livingston shook his head. ''You amaze me, partner. You read all of that from a bunch of dirt. I never was much of a tracker. Lucky for me that I found you, huh?''

Shaking his head, Anderson smiled. But thoughts of the girl with those murderers quickly transformed that grin to a frown. He looked at the sun, disappearing beneath the mountain range to the west.

The former deputy read his partner's mind. ''Not much use in moving on,'' he said. ''We can't track them at night, so I say we take advantage of the cabin.''

Anderson agreed, and the two put their horses and Breckenridge's mule in the corral. They rubbed down the animals and gave them oats and water before walking toward the cabin.

Livingston stopped at the door and motioned to Anderson with a bow, saying, ''After you, partner.''

Wesley Anderson's reply was drowned out by a gunshot.

''I still got concerns about our back trail,'' Lane Morris said after making sure the ropes securing the Breckenridge girl were tight. He took a seat by the fire, fished the whetstone out of his saddlebags, and began honing his massive bowie knife.

Major Vaughn MacDermott swallowed a bite of beef jerky and began rolling a cigarette. ''I've told you, the back trail is covered. You just concentrate on the trail ahead and the girl.''

''Yeah,'' Morris said. ''But I still don't like it.''

''I don't care what you like. I'm running this gang.''

Not that it's much of a gang, MacDermott thought as he struck a match against the butt of one of his revolvers and lit a smoke. Ten to twelve years ago, he and Lee Thorn had commanded twenty men, taking anything they cared to. Then Thorn had gone around the bend, turned crazy, and the vigilantes starting dogging their trail.

When he hit Dunbar's party back in '73, he had everything planned to perfection. It would be his last raid in Wyoming Territory. He would take most of the gold for himself and light a shuck south, maybe Texas, Mexico, or even South America, where he could live like a king.

But it didn't turn out that way. He had a fortune in gold at his fingertips, only to lose it to his loco partner. And now, four years later, instead of living on a tropical hacienda or leading an army of outlaws, he had this. He took a long drag of his cigarette and stared at Lane Morris, that knife-wielding maniac who had become his top lieutenant. Morris was a survivor from the old gang, but there was no closeness between the two. The only thing Morris ever befriended was that bowie knife he kept razor sharp. Then there was Keno, a pockmarked simpleton who had murdered at least two miners for the gold fillings in their teeth.

MacDermott sighed and flicked his cigarette into the fire. His gaze turned toward Cora Breckenridge, and he thought about the gold, that fortune that would buy him that place in Mexico, and maybe another—a good—army of outlaws so that he could add to his wealth.

Louie Chapman levered his Winchester rifle and fired several shots into the Breckenridge cabin against his better judgment. He had ordered Wert Pierce not to fire, but the fool had shot anyway, missing no doubt, and the two men had taken cover in the log building. Wert's two friends, Mifflin and the Mexican Lazo, had joined the fracas, burning powder and shot with little effect. The Breckenridge cabin was built like an ironclad.

Finally Chapman lowered his rifle and yelled, ''Stop

shooting! Hold your fire!'' Several more shots sounded before Wert and the others stopped and turned toward the aging bartender.

"I had that gunman in my sights," Wert said. "Had him dead to rights. Lousy gun must shoot high!" He tossed the battered Spencer rifle to the ground.

"Now what?" Mifflin asked. "We give it up, go back to town?"

Louie Chapman had no intention of going back to Fort Bourbon. Not when he was this close to Dunbar's treasure. For all he knew, the stranger and deputy had the gold right now in that dead miner's cabin. The sun was sinking fast, and Chapman figured they could get closer under the cover of darkness, maybe burn them out at first light, although he didn't want to risk a fire with all that gold to be had.

Maybe, he thought with a grin, he could talk Wert and the other two into charging into the cabin and killing the two men inside. With any luck, Wert and his friends would also be shot dead.

"As soon as it gets dark, we'll move in closer for the kill," Chapman said. "Pick up your rifle, Wert, and reload it. Those two aren't going anywhere."

Wesley Anderson was on his knees, his hands balled into fists, trying to get the dirt from his eyes. He heard the reports of several rifles but Paul Livingston had not returned fire.

The first bullet had struck above the door to the cabin, sending a ton of dirt and maybe some splinters into Anderson's face. His reflexes had taken over, however, and he dived inside, followed by his new partner, who kicked the door shut and barred it. Anderson groaned, his Navy at his feet, but gradually his vision returned. Bullets whacked against the door and log walls. But there was only one window in the cabin, and it was in the back facing west, away from the ambushers, protected by a closed shutter.

After a few minutes, Anderson felt as if he could see well enough to shoot, so he picked up his Colt and stood near the door. Livingston was crouched, rocking on his heels, his rifle cradled across his thighs. He was silent, listening intently at the gunshots outside.

"Figure they doubled back on us?" Anderson asked.

Livingston looked thunderstruck as the color drained from his face. "No," he said with a gasp. "No, it couldn't be." He was silent again, listening, but the gunfire slowly died and Livingston took a deep breath and sighed as his color returned.

"I'm guessing four men," he said. "We were trailing three, you said. So I think we have a new batch of gold-seekers."

Anderson took a deep breath. "I thought you said the curse and all of those stories had scared off the fortune-hunters."

"I did. And it was true. But I reckon you got some people interested again." Livingston looked at Anderson's revolver and shook his head. "We're up against four rifles. That short gun of yours isn't going to help us at all from this range."

"Then I guess I'll just have to get closer," Anderson said.

At full dark, Anderson opened the shutter and

peered into the blackness. He pulled himself onto the sill, paused for a second, and dropped to the ground silently, crouching by the wall and cocking the .36. Livingston followed, cradling his rifle, and the two waited as their eyes adjusted to the darkness.

Wes moved slowly to the edge of the cabin, listened for half a minute, then sprinted to the corral. He stopped at the post, looking toward the hill where the riflemen had opened up on the cabin. He ducked underneath the low rail and moved inside the fence. One of the horses snorted, and he stopped, holding his breath. Before he took another step, he heard the voices and quickly, but silently, planted his body on the cold earth.

Men were walking from the shed, mumbling softly, and Anderson could make out the sloshing of a bucket.

"How we do this?" a Mexican voice asked no more than ten yards in front of him.

"I'll throw the coal oil on the door and you fire it up. Them boys will come runnin' out to die game or burn like Ma's brisket."

"Let me light my cigar now," the Mexican said.

"Be quick about it, Lazo."

Anderson raised his arm, aiming the Colt at the voices. These ambushers weren't the smartest men in Wyoming, and they would pay for their stupidity. The match flared, illuminating the Mexican's mustached face. Wesley waited and adjusted his aim as the flame grew while the man puffed on his cigar.

"Hey!" he yelled and pulled the trigger, rolling to his left while simultaneously thumbing back the hammer on his Colt. The night went black immediately as the bandit named Lazo staggered back, dropping his bucket of coal oil and cigar. A muzzle flash blinked nearby, the bullet whining into the corral, and Anderson snapped off a shot at the brief flame, knowing he had missed.

Horses squealed, and the ground suddenly caught fire. It took a few seconds for Wes to realize that the Mexican's cigar or match had ignited the spilled oil. He had a clear view now as he leaned against the fence post, stretched out his right arm, and searched for his attackers. He spotted the Mexican motionless on the ground, and saw the other man backing up toward the cabin, away from the flames. The man found Anderson and fired, splintering the top rail over the young man's head.

"Wert!" the man shouted, and Wesley shot him in the gut.

Anderson breathed again and moved to the corner of the corral. Two men were down, but at least two others remained. The flames spread toward the corral, fed by the dry grass, as Wes looked past the fire toward the hills, but he could make out nothing fifty feet away. He started to climb out of the corral when he heard the metallic click of a rifle being cocked.

He spun around and recognized a face ten feet away—Wert, the bad-tempered miner at Fort Bourbon. Wes was pinned against the corral fence, so he fought the natural instinct to dive to his left and instead leaned forward and fell directly toward the man as his rifle boomed.

The muzzle blast burned the Texan's back, and the miner swore. He had missed, anticipating that Anderson would move left. Wes pulled the trigger, cocked the revolver, and rolled over. The miner had levered another round into his Spencer and was drawing a careful bead on Wesley. A rifle shot cracked, and Wert staggered back against the fence, dropping the Spencer and groaning. Another shot tore through the miner's chest, and Wert dropped silently to the ground, tried to rise once, and collapsed with a sigh.

Anderson glanced at the dead miner, sucked in smoky air, and watched as Paul Livingston rounded the cabin, jacking another cartridge into his Henry. He held up his left hand, flashing one finger and nodding toward the hills.

One man remained, and Anderson heard the sound of hooves. A figure galloped into the yard, reining to a hard stop just beyond the fire. The man shot quickly at Livingston. Wesley fired from his hip and saw the rider clutch his left shoulder and send the rifle falling to the ground. The man swore, gathered his reins, and turned the horse around, loping toward the hills. Livingston raised his Henry and fired at the fleeing figure, now merely a shadow. The man screamed and fell to the ground as the horse continued its sprint back toward South Pass.

Anderson glared at Livingston as he ducked under the rails and came out of the corral. "It took you long enough," he said dryly, shoving the Colt into his holster.

Livingston smiled. "Partner, Wert Pierce had you dead to rights. You'd be a dead man if it weren't for me."

There was no arguing that point, so Anderson

grabbed a saddle blanket straddling the fence and began beating out the grass fire. A shot boomed in the darkness, and Wes spun around, whipping out the Colt and staring in disbelief at his partner. Paul Livingston, the former deputy marshal of South Pass City, had just shot one of the ambushers—the man Wes had gutshot—in the head.

"What are you doing?" Wes cried out.

Livingston turned, chambering another round and stepping toward the Mexican. "Wes, you need to grow up. You think these boys would give us any quarter if it were the other way around?" Before the Texan could respond, Livingston had placed the muzzle on Lazo's forehead and pulled the trigger.

"I don't have the time or inclination to haul off a bunch of prisoners," Paul continued, "and I'm not about to take any chances of having one of these boys play possum and shoot me in the back."

Livingston ducked into the corral and moved toward Wert. Anderson took a deep breath, palmed his revolver, and walked past the dying fire to find the final bushwhacker. He heard Livingston's Henry bark its coup de grâce on Pierce long before he reached the prostrate man on the hillside.

Anderson kicked the man once, then knelt beside him and struck a match, holding the lucifer close to the face. It was the bartender from South Pass, Louie, still alive. His shoulder was soaked in blood, and his left arm was shattered. The old man said nothing, but his face was masked in pain. Wesley heard Livingston's boots behind him, so he stood quickly, aimed at the bartender and pulled the trigger. He turned and walked away.

"He dead?" Livingston asked.

"He is now," Anderson replied.

"Good. Let's saddle up and put a couple of miles behind us. This place doesn't seem quite as inviting as it did earlier."

Wesley nodded and followed the rifleman toward the corral, wondering just what kind of man he had chosen for a partner.

Chapter Five

Louie Chapman awoke at dawn, cold and tired. His left arm was numb, but the bleeding seemed to have stopped. He slowly pulled himself to his knees and looked at the Breckenridge claim. Mifflin and Lazo lay near the blackened grass by the cabin. Pierce was facedown in the corral.

By all rights, Louie should be dead too. That shaggy-haired Texan had popped a cap at point-blank range, but the bullet dug into the soil by Chapman's right ear. He had missed on purpose, then lied to that slick-talking lawman before the two had ridden out.

Chapman studied his options and realized he had no choice but to start walking back to town. Maybe he would find his horse, or one of his men's that had bolted during the gunfight. Dunbar's gold wasn't at Breckenridge's cabin. That was for certain. Perhaps Livingston and that kid would find it. More than likely they would die.

With a groan, Chapman stood and glanced at his mangled arm. Dunbar's gold. It was cursed, he decided. Louie had been one of the fortunate seekers. He was still alive, though as bad as his arm and shoulder looked, he wasn't sure he'd live to see South Pass City. Either way, he was finished with Alec Dunbar's fortune.

Jonathan Vaughn MacDermott kicked Cora Breckenridge awake. "Get up," he said, "and get ready to ride." He turned quickly and went to the horses, where Keno and Morris were saddling up.

Cora rolled to a sitting position on her bed of pine needles, then slowly brought her hands, bound tightly with a piece of rawhide, to her face. She winced as she touched a dark bruise below her left eye and stared at her kidnappers.

MacDermott had beaten her, the man called Keno had tied her and roughly thrown her on the horse, but it was the third one, Lane Morris, she feared most. He was lean and leathery, with dark, malevolent eyes. Morris was MacDermott's right-hand man, had murdered more times than she could count, and from the way he kept honing the big bowie knife he carried on his hip, she knew he would have no qualms about killing her.

She stood slowly, awkwardly, and her stomach growled. She had not eaten since breakfast the day before—and that seemed like weeks ago. A bird called, and she heard a creek flowing nearby. Cora looked around, bit her lip, and tried to think of a way to escape. They were beginning to climb into the mountains, and the heavy forest offered plenty of places to hide if she could only get a head start and somehow cut the rawhide around her wrists.

"Girl!" MacDermott shouted. "I said get a move on!"

The morning wind was biting, and Wesley Anderson was glad he had bought the mackinaw coat in South Pass City. He swung from his horse, picked up a broken twig, and studied the ground a minute longer. A few feet ahead he saw some horse manure.

"They're not worried about leaving sign," he finally said.

"Likely don't expect to be followed," Livingston quickly offered, and the pack animal behind him snorted as if it agreed.

Anderson rubbed his hands together and thought. It didn't make much sense. The killers left Breckenridge's body in town, sure to be found, kidnapped his daughter, and ransacked their cabin. They had to know someone would leave South Pass City to tell his daughter or bring his body out for burial. Maybe, he thought, they didn't care if they were followed. Not many outlaws were that brazen. Jesse James and Cole Younger, maybe. Vaughn MacDermott, perhaps.

After mounting his horse, Anderson looked at the graying clouds and pulled up his collar. "Now isn't a real good time to be climbing into these mountains."

Livingston laughed. "For one hundred thousand in gold, I wouldn't be too concerned about a little cold." Then he cackled. "Hey, that rhymes. I'm a poet!"

Shaking his head, Anderson kicked his horse into a trot.

Cora rode with her head down. MacDermott and Keno followed slightly behind her with the pack mule trailing them; Morris had gone off ahead to scout. For that she was glad. A blanket of pine needles paved the trail, if it could be called that, and she remembered the first time her father brought her up here.

She must have been twelve, maybe only eleven, and she had slept under the stars, eaten jerked venison, made scalding coffee for breakfast, and given names to all the landmarks: Elk Fork for the split in the trail where she had seen a herd grazing; Calvary Hill for a rise with three dead pines that resembled crosses; and Gunsight Pass for the narrow gap in the mountains with a snow-capped peak in the distance that looked like a rifle bead.

Her saddle creaked and Cora concentrated. Her father had traded with a Texas cowboy for the saddle, a fancy number with Mexican conchos that Cora detested. Her father thought it was pretty; Cora called it tacky, but now she was grateful for the conchos. One was attached to the saddle horn, and for the past few hours Cora had been rubbing the rawhide thong against it, careful so that MacDermott wouldn't notice.

Finally the thong broke. That was the easy part, she thought. She had better make her move now, before Morris returned.

Keeping her wrists together, pretending they were still tied, she raised her arms to push a pine branch in front of her, then, biting her lip, listening to the horses behind her, she let go of the branch and kicked her dun hard. The branch snapped back like a scythe, catching MacDermott full in the face. He groaned and toppled from the saddle as Keno's mount reared.

Cora grabbed the reins and leaned forward as she zigzagged through the trees and brush that lined the trail. She heard the retort of a pistol as something zipped past her ear. MacDermott yelled, "Don't kill her, you fool! Get her!"

She kicked the dun harder and leaned lower.

"What's your interest in the girl?" Anderson asked as they slowly followed the mountain trail.

The question came from an ambush, and Livingston was slow to reply. "Strictly professional. I've seen her a time or two, knew her father a little."

Anderson snorted. "You seem to know a lot about her."

"I hope you aren't getting jealous, friend," Livingston said, laughing. "I barely know the girl. And you don't know her at all."

"Uh-huh," Anderson grunted, pretending to study the ground. It wasn't really necessary because anyone could follow the trail the killers were leaving. He was more interested in his new partner, and the more he thought about it, the less he liked the entire situation: Livingston's clothes were too expensive for an honest deputy, but then, a lot of mining-camp lawmen took cuts from the gambling establishments. And he seemed to know more about the Breckenridges than he let on. Not to mention MacDermott.

"Don't fret too much over the girl," Livingston

said. "From what I know about Cora, she can take care of herself."

The dun rounded the bend sharply and slammed into something solid, pitching Cora from her saddle and into a fallen tree. The breath left her lungs and she gasped for air, slowly realizing that her horse had collided with another horse. She panicked, knowing it was Lane Morris.

Cora found her feet and stumbled forward, tears streaming from pain and terror. Morris was running behind her, panting in the thin air, but steadily gaining, and she knew she could not outrun him. She screamed as she felt his breath against her neck, then his hand grabbed her shoulder.

Suddenly, she was on her back, gasping, staring into Morris's unforgiving eyes.

The killer smiled without humor as he drew the big, lethal bowie from its sheath. He knelt over her, and using the point of knife, traced up her chest. Next the point was at her throat, pressing harder, and she clenched her fists and closed her eyes.

"Lane," a voice called. "She's no good to us dead. Don't make the same mistake twice."

Slowly Morris straightened and sheathed the knife. Cora opened her eyes and saw Vaughn MacDermott, bleeding slightly from a cut below his left eye. She took silent satisfaction in that little bit of revenge for the bruise he had given her.

Morris walked past MacDermott to the horses. Cora awkwardly found her feet, then stumbled, but Mac-Dermott caught her. "You gonna be all right?" he asked, and his concern seemed genuine. When she didn't answer, MacDermott added, ''All I want is the gold. All you have to do is get us to Gunsight Pass, help us find your father's mountain camp, and I'll send you on your way.

''I have never popped a cap on any woman, and I don't intend to start now, but Lane and Keno, they don't care. They'll kill anyone. And I can't look after you if you try to escape.'' He let her go and waited for her to answer.

He was like a beer tap, she thought. He could turn on the kindness or anger, then shut it off in an instant.

''I'll see you dead,'' she said.

Shaking his head, MacDermott led her to the dun and shoved her into the saddle. *They think I'm giving up,* she thought, and took advantage of the situation. Her left boot shot out and struck MacDermott in the sternum, and she shrieked, startling the outlaws' horses, and galloped through the forest again.

She made it less than five hundred yards before the trail ended in front of a thicket of dead trees and brambles and a moss-covered chunk of granite. Cora dropped to the ground and sprinted through the forest. Branches and vines popped her face until she tripped over a root and stumbled into a clearing, falling headfirst onto damp leaves.

Her chest heaved, and as she tried to rise, she saw the pair of moccasins barely a yard from her face. The leather had been dyed red and decorated with yellow and blue beads and porcupine quills. Cora lifted her head and saw the Indian, sitting on a rotting stump, staring past her with dark, expressionless eyes.

He was ancient, with a weathered, round, dark face. His silver hair was swept up in the front, with long braids, bounded by white rawhide, falling to his waist. A deerskin shirt, the color of a pink salmon, was unadorned except for a collar of otter skin, its tail hanging down the front, and he wore black leggings and a long, plaid breechcloth. The Indian sat with his arms folded, and if he thought anything of Cora, he didn't show it.

She heard the sounds of footsteps, and tried to move. But Vaughn MacDermott grabbed a fistful of her hair and pushed her face into the dead leaves.

He swore, gasped for breath, and released her hair. Cora rolled over, frightened, but saw both outlaws staring at the old Indian. She thought briefly about running, but realized escape was fruitless, so she brought her knees up under her chin and waited.

"Who are you?" MacDermott snapped at the Indian, but the old-timer did not respond.

"Lane."

Morris stepped forward and barked out, *"Ne-toneseve?"* Still no answer. *"Ne-tsehese-nestse-he?"* Cora recognized the glottal words as Cheyenne, but this man was no Cheyenne. Even she realized that from his hair, the upswept style she remembered seeing in a photograph of Chief Joseph.

"He's Nez Percé," she said, adding, "I think."

The old man's black eyes fell briefly on Cora before returning to look into nothing. MacDermott considered this a moment. There had been trouble with the Nez Percé this summer up north when Chief Joseph led his people from the reservation on a wild flight after some of his braves massacred several folks in Idaho. MacDermott had picked up most of his information from newspapers and third- and fourth-hand sources.

The Indians and the Army had fought at Big Hole in Montana, even cut through Yellowstone National Park in Wyoming last month, but the last he heard, the Nez Percé were on their way to Canada to join Sitting Bull and his Sioux, and had just cut through the Crow Reservation on Clarks Fork River, a far piece from here.

"If he's Nez Percé, he's a long ways from home," Lane Morris said.

MacDermott shook his head. "I've heard of Indians dumping their old, leaving them to go in the woods and die," he said. "I expect they left this codger on the Yellowstone, only he ain't died yet, and he's been walking south since."

"Well," Morris said, and drew his knife. "He ain't walkin' no further. I aim to add a Nez Percé scalp to my collection."

The killer laughed and walked confidently to the Indian. But as soon as Morris gripped the old man's thick pompadour with his left hand, the Nez Percé smiled and said in perfect English:

"If you kill me, you will never find the cave the Crow call the Lair Which Weeps."

Chapter Six

His name was Hohops, and he carried no weapon or food, only an eagle wing. He said he was a *tewat*, a holy man, who could read what will be by studying Mother Earth. Lane Morris swore loudly and laughed, but MacDermott contemplated the Nez Percé and ordered him to accompany them back to camp.

Cora hadn't realized how skinny the old man was until he sat down beside her and stuffed his mouth with stale biscuits and jerked beef. His skin was tight against the bones in his arms, and his fingers seemed more skeletal than flesh. He washed down his food with bitter coffee, nodded politely, and stared ahead at MacDermott, Morris, and Keno, who eyed him curiously but suspiciously.

"All right," MacDermott said, "now that you've filled your belly, you're gonna answer some questions, Mr. Hohops."

The medicine man said nothing.

"How do you know we seek the Lair Which Weeps?"

Hohops bent forward and filled his right hand with dirt, lifted it to his waist, and let the granules slip through his bony fingers and sprinkle his moccasins.

"Mother Earth," he said, "knows all. We are born of Earth, and when we die, the Earth claims us again. She holds all of our secrets, all of our answers. I know how to read those secrets, those answers." He closed his eyes, raised the eagle wing to cover his eyes and nose, and began singing, more like chanting, some haunting song in the Nez Percé tongue.

While he was singing, Lane Morris spit a stream of tobacco juice into the fire and muttered an oath.

When his song was finished, Hohops lowered the shield and stared ahead. MacDermott scratched his nose. "The Lair Which Weeps," the major said, "is far from the Nez Percé reservation. How do you know of this place?"

"The Cheyenne know of the cave," Hohops said, "and this is not Cheyenne land. The Shoshone, Lakota, even the Bannock are familiar with the evil place. I know it better than all because my spirit guards the lair."

"You're a liar," Morris said.

Cora could barely believe what she saw. In an instant, Hohops was on top of Morris, his thin, brittle hands gripping the killer's throat with such intensity that even MacDermott and Keno couldn't pull the man off. Finally, MacDermott drew a revolver, pressed the barrel against the Indian's temple, and ordered him to back off. "Do it!" MacDermott swore and cocked the revolver. "Do it now, or I'll kill you!"

Hohops released the gunman and backed away, folded his arms, and sat beside Cora. Morris sat up quickly, gasping for breath while reaching for his knife, but MacDermott stopped him.

"Ease up, Lane. You know better than calling an Indian a liar."

"I'll kill him!"

"Not now you won't. Go get a bottle. A little whiskey'll help your throat. But you leave Mr. Hohops alone. For now."

He lowered the Colt and smiled at the Nez Percé, found his seat, and asked, "How do you know we seek this cave?"

"You wish to find the yellow iron you murdered for. The gold you seek is there."

"How do you know this?"

"I have seen it."

MacDermott licked his lips. "You can lead us there?"

Hohops nodded, and a bony finger pointed to Cora. "And she also knows the way. Her father, the man he"—the Indian nodded toward Morris—"killed against your orders in the white man's town that is found toward the rising sun had discovered the cave. She has memories of the place and can take you close to its location. I can then lead you to its opening."

"Don't trust him, Vaughn," Morris shot out. "It's some kind of trick. How else would he know that I killed that old fool?"

Hohops smiled and shook his head as he again lifted

a handful of dirt, which he tossed into the air. "Believe me or don't, but if you harm me or the girl, you will never find the precious metal that you seek."

MacDermott suddenly laughed. "You want a cut of the gold, don't you?"

Hohops shook his head. "The People turned me loose to die, for I would be a hindrance to them as they try to join our Lakota friends in the Grandmother's Country. And I shall die and return to the Mother Earth that tells and knows all. I shall pass over the mountain near the cave where my spirit waits. No, *kap-seese*, I have no use for your blood money. You will have no need of it either."

Cora looked at MacDermott, who rubbed the back of his right hand against his day-old beard stubble. She didn't know what to make of the Nez Percé medicine man. Cora had never seen him before—of this she was certain—but Hohops knew about her father's murder, knew he had once brought her into these hills to Gunsight Pass and had more than just a passing familiarity with the legend of Alec Dunbar's fortune and Major Jonathan Vaughn MacDermott's ruthlessness. Could the man really read the future and past in nothing more than dirt?

"Kap-seese," Hohops said. "If you do not believe me now, maybe this will convince you. Before the sun sinks lower, you will have visitors that neither you nor I wish to see."

MacDermott barked a quick order, and Keno scurried up a ledge and studied the trail. He had been up there less than five minutes when he swore and shouted at MacDermott: "Major, that old-timer's right! Posse, and they're headin' right toward us!"

Wes looked at the tracks briefly and, with a shrug, pulled himself back into the saddle. "They're in no hurry," he told his partner and repeated his concern about climbing into the mountains. "And they should be. The last place I'd want to get caught in a snowstorm is up in these mountains."

Livingston laughed. "Spoken like a true Texan. Wes, I would have thought your blood would be a lot thicker after, what, a dozen or so years up here and four of those in the 'Big House.' " The Mississippian shook his head and unsuccessfully tried to stifle a yawn. "They can't move as fast as we can. We'll catch up with them quickly."

"And then?"

"Rescue Cora, of course. Kill the others, and then we'll continue on to find Dunbar's fortune. I'm not greedy, Wes. We'll split it even between you, me, and Cora. Does that sound fair?"

Anderson nodded.

There was a glint in Livingston's eyes. "You sure, partner? I mean, gold—especially that much gold— can turn a man nasty."

Wesley shook his head and said, "Not me," but as he rode ahead, he thought about his answer.

For four years, he had thought often about Dunbar's treasure, about what he would do with one hundred thousand dollars. He had convinced himself that Wyoming Territory owed him the money. In places like the South Pass district, Bannack City in Montana, and the gold fields of Colorado, he had seen what greed could do to men. They would lie, steal, and kill for gold. For some, it was an obsession that tormented them. Gold had led men to sanitariums, prisons, the gallows, and graveyards. He wouldn't become like them, he thought. *I can handle this,* he told himself.

But sometimes he wasn't so sure.

He heard the noise then, far in the distance but carried by the wind. Livingston reined in his horse and listened intently, mouth open. Gunfire. A lot of it. The noise lasted less than two minutes, then died with the breeze.

The former deputy smiled and kicked his horse forward. "Maybe," he told Anderson, "we won't have to kill Cora's kidnappers. Somebody might have done that chore for us."

MacDermott cut loose the rawhide thong binding Cora's wrists with a pocketknife and sat beside her, pulling a woolen blanket over both their bodies as if they were newlyweds. He smiled, called her "honey," and poked her in the ribs with the barrel of one of his Colts, hidden beneath the blanket.

"Just play along, Mrs. Mousiness," he said. "We're just a couple searchin' for gold."

Keno and Morris had disappeared in the thicket, and they had taken Hohops with them. There had been no time to run from the posse, or set up a better ambush, so MacDermott just waited as the riders slowly entered the clearing.

It was an Army patrol, not a civilian posse from town as she had expected. Six men in dirty blue uniforms and bearded faces halted their worn-out mounts a few yards from the campfire. One man with angry eyes and a reddish brown beard removed his gauntlets and stared at MacDermott and Cora. His dirty blouse carried the insignia of a Cavalry lieutenant. The other men were only privates.

The gunman smiled and yawned, stretching his left arm above his head. "Howdy," he said. "Cora, honey, why don't you see if these soldiers need some coffee."

She was glad to get away from MacDermott and quickly crawled from underneath the blanket and walked to the coffeepot.

"No thanks," the lieutenant said, and Cora read the disappointment in his troopers' eyes. They must have been in the saddle for days.

"What can I do for you then?" MacDermott asked, his gun hand still underneath the blanket. "Forgive me if I don't rise, but we've been looking for Dunbar's gold all day, and I'm just plumb tuckered out. I'm John Mousiness from Atlantic City. This here is my concubine, Cora."

She glared at him, and her face reddened when one of the soldiers snickered. MacDermott's eyes danced with amusement.

"Second Lieutenant Donald Glass, First United States Cavalry," the officer said, "at your service. We're trying to gather up any Nez Percé who fled south since the fight at Big Hole." The man sounded bitter about his orders.

"That's a shame, Lieutenant," MacDermott said. "The odds of getting a brevet nurse-maiding some dying old Indians aren't as good as they would be if you were chasing old Chief Joseph with the rest of your boys.'' He smiled and added, for spite, ''Are they?''

Cora stepped away from the fire, backing toward the picketed animals. MacDermott was going out of his way to pick a fight with the soldiers when all he had to do was cooperate briefly and send them on their way.

''I take it you haven't seen any Indians, Mr. Mousiness,'' Glass said.

Clucking his tongue, MacDermott slowly shook his head.

''And you just happen to have a Nez Percé ceremonial eagle wing in your camp?''

MacDermott glanced at the item Hohops had left on the ground. With a bemused expression, he shook his head, snorted, and shot the lieutenant in the forehead.

The answering gunfire was deafening, and Cora dropped to her knees and covered her ears with both hands. Horses screamed over the roar of rifles and revolvers and whine of lead. She saw the lieutenant topple from his horse, and bullets raked the other soldiers as they tried to dismount and lift their weapons.

MacDermott leaped to his feet, thumbed back the hammer of his Colt, and killed another trooper while Keno and Morris fired their rifles from the brush. Suddenly, a piercing cry like a hawk cut through the air, and Cora watched as Hohops charged into the ambushed patrol. The old man ducked underneath a rearing horse and slapped the dead lieutenant's head with a dead limb he had picked up off the ground.

''I've counted coup!'' Hohops shouted. *''Yi-hell-*

lis!'' He hit the dead man again, and touched another soldier.

A shot dropped the rearing horse, throwing the soldier against a pine. Hohops poked the trooper with his stick just before bullets riddled the young man's body. Five men were down, and the remaining trooper tried to gallop out of the camp, but a gunshot thudded in his back and sent him crashing to the ground while his horse galloped down the trail.

The smell of black powder and blood sickened Cora. With her ears still ringing, she fought back nausea as she stared at the bodies of the six dead Army men and three dying horses. The two other mounts had sprinted up the trail. MacDermott shucked the empty brass casings from his revolver and reloaded his Colt while Morris and Keno crawled out of their hiding places.

Hohops, the strange Nez Percé, stood gloating over the bloody bodies of the soldiers. ''I hate the bluecoats, killers of my people,'' he told MacDermott, ''almost as much as I hate you.'' Smiling, he walked past the outlaw leader and picked up his eagle wing.

''Keno,'' MacDermott said, nodding at the soldiers, ''make sure they're all dead.''

Cora closed her eyes and mumbled a prayer.

''Major MacDermott,'' she heard Hohops ask, ''now do you believe in my power?''

Chapter Seven

Drawing his Colt, Wes Anderson dismounted and walked into the clearing. He glanced briefly at the body of the soldier near the trail and moved toward the other dead. Six men and three horses had stained the ground with blood, and Wes was grateful that the wind blew hard, carrying the stench of death downhill. Anderson squatted by the remains of a campfire, picked up the empty brass shells from a .45 and considered these a moment before holding his hand over the ashes. They were still warm.

"All them Yankees dead?" Paul Livingston asked.

Anderson nodded. He didn't tell his partner that every soldier had also been shot once in the head, probably after they were dead, meaning someone else in these parts followed Livingston's barbaric practice.

"I'll stay out here until you're finished reading the sign," Paul said. "Don't want to mess up anything."

Wes nodded. Reading this ground, piecing together

61

what had happened by inching over the ground would prove difficult. The place was a mess. After the gunfight, Cora's kidnappers had left in a hurry. Still, he examined the camp carefully, studying the brass casings, bullet holes, snapped branches, and cigarette ends.

One man, with the .45-caliber revolver, had greeted the soldiers. Shortly thereafter, he started shooting, and two others opened up with their rifles from a spot twenty yards from the center of camp. Apparently, the Cavalrymen were not expecting gunplay because the troopers hadn't even gotten off one shot. Afterward, the murderers had ridden away, leaving the bodies for the wolves and the guns to be claimed by rust.

He learned all of this while keeping the Colt in his hand, not wanting to be caught by surprise, the way these soldiers had been.

A horse snorted, and Anderson looked up the trail. An exhausted dun stood, head down, McClellan's saddle hanging underneath its belly. Wes made out the "US" brand on the animal's flank.

"Take care of that horse, Paul," he said, and his partner nodded.

Livingston and Anderson had passed one terrified Army mount on the way up. Three others lay dead. That meant one remained. Slowly Wesley began to interpret the rest of the story out of the ground as he followed hoofprints and markings from bootheels out of the clearing, saw where the killers had mounted and loped up the trail. There was an extra horse now. He guessed that they took the remaining animal with them.

Wes paused and fingered a small depression in the dirt. He looked closer. A moccasin? Yes. A fourth man had mounted the Army horse and ridden with them.

"Someone else has joined the party," Anderson said and looked up at Livingston.

Paul had removed the saddle and bridle off the dun and now walked to where Anderson knelt. Wes pointed out the moccasin print and explained what it was.

"Scout with the Army patrol?" Paul guessed.

Wes shook his head. "Only six horses rode in. This man was with them in camp."

Livingston chewed on the knuckle of his right thumb. "That's strange." There was no sense in trying to figure out where the new man came from, though. They'd find the answer to that question when they caught up with them.

"How much time do they have on us?" Paul asked.

"A few hours at the most."

"Well, let's get a move on and join their little party."

"We should bury these men," Anderson said.

Livingston scoffed at the suggestion. "Yankees? Not on your life."

Anderson rose without speaking, holstered his Colt, and walked to the pack animal, where he unfastened a shovel.

"Wes, we don't have time for this," Livingston pleaded. "We didn't bury those men at Breckenridge's cabin—"

"Those men tried to kill us," Wesley said, "and it

was night. These soldiers were murdered, and we have plenty of daylight.''

Livingston sighed wearily, but his eyes flamed with anger when Anderson suddenly tossed him the shovel.

Paul let the shovel drop by his feet. ''I ain't about to bury no Yankee. Not after what they put me through in Vicksburg.''

Wes smiled. Livingston had left his Henry in the saddle scabbard, and Anderson knew his partner was no match against him with a short gun. ''It'll go faster if we both dig,'' Anderson said.

He felt the tension, but Wesley wasn't scared. He was in the right. They should have buried the men back at the cabin, and he wasn't going to make the same mistake again. Would Paul draw on him? Anderson wasn't sure. Another shovel was tied on the other side of the pack, but Anderson wouldn't move for it until his partner relented.

Anderson waited, and after a minute, he saw the corners of Paul's lips turn upward.

''Well,'' Livingston finally said, ''since you have such a conscience, I'll give you this one. But it's gonna cost you, say, a couple ounces of Dunbar's gold.''

''Now who's greedy?'' Anderson said, and Livingston laughed as he bent down to pick up the shovel.

Keno tightened the rawhide around Cora's wrists until she gasped and dropped a scratchy woolen blanket over her ankles, which he had also tied together with a rope and secured to a tree trunk. Next, he moved purposefully to Hohops on the other side of the campfire.

"Stick 'em out," the outlaw ordered, and the Indian complied without comment as Keno tied Hohops's hands and backed away.

MacDermott smiled. "I wish we didn't have to do that, friends, but it's a simple precaution. I don't trust you." He began rolling a cigarette and nodded at Keno. "You've got guard duty," he ordered.

"Sleep well, tonight," Hohops said, staring at his feet.

Cora didn't know whom the Indian was talking to. She looked at him briefly before pulling the blanket over her shoulders and closing her eyes, fighting back tears, not realizing how exhausted she was as she drifted off to sleep.

Anderson brought out his pennywhistle and began playing. The notes floated from the instrument and hung over the camp like fog, a haunting, eerie sound in the darkness of their cold camp. It was a sad song, a lament, something he had made up while leaning against a cold prison wall. He only played it when he was worried.

"How 'bout something a little livelier, partner," Livingston said when the last notes drifted away. "Like a funeral dirge."

Anderson started *Dixie*, then abruptly stopped and stood, peering into the darkness. Livingston jumped up and grabbed his Henry rifle. "What is it?" he asked, looking in the distance, trying to follow where

Anderson pointed. At last he saw it, a flicker of light, from a campfire, only a few miles away.

Wes wrapped the pennywhistle and slid it into his boot, feeling like a fool for playing music when they were trailing a bunch of killers. Noise traveled far in these hills, especially at night.

"Got to be them," Livingston said. "Let's go." He turned and walked toward the picketed horses and mule.

"You have a plan?" Anderson called, and Livingston stopped. "First thing we have to do is get that girl out safely," Anderson added.

Livingston sighed, frowned, and took a deep breath. Within seconds, however, he was smiling again. "Something's bound to come to me before we get there."

They had picketed their animals a half-mile back and silently made their way to the edge of camp. Hiding behind a tree, Livingston and Anderson surveyed the surroundings. "Good thing we didn't build a fire tonight," Livingston whispered. "They might have smelled our woodsmoke."

Anderson wasn't listening. He studied the camp, saw the girl in her bedroll at the edge of the clearing, the horses and mule picketed off to the side. Two men were sleeping near the campfire and a third sat at the other edge of camp, across from the girl, leaning against a pine and smoking a cigarette. A fourth figure lay opposite the girl. Four against two, but it was a starless, moonless night, and apparently the killers didn't think they were being followed. Why else would they have only one sentry and a campfire so big?

"Well?" Anderson asked.

Livingston pointed to the girl. "You slip down there, wake her, don't let her scream, then cut her loose with that pocketknife of yours, get her into the trees, and keep her head down. As soon as you're out, I'll cut loose at them from up here with the Henry. That campfire will make it easy. They'll have to give up or get ready to knock on St. Paul's door."

"St. Peter's gate," Anderson corrected. "What about the guard?"

"He's your problem," Livingston said. "You should be able to get behind him, either bash in the side of his head with your Navy or slit his throat. Just don't let him wake the others."

"And if they wake up anyway?"

Livingston smiled. "Don't worry, partner. I've got you covered."

Anderson took a deep breath, slowly let it out, then began picking his way to the camp.

An owl hooted as Anderson crawled silently. Logs popped in the fire and he stopped, looking around. The Navy Colt was in his right hand, the closed pocket-knife clenched tightly in his left. He realized he was sweating despite the night chill.

In front of him, the sentry leaned against the pine. Anderson could see the man's legs, boots, and a sack of Bull Durham tobacco. After slowly rising to his feet, Anderson carefully approached him. He knew he couldn't cut a man's throat as Livingston had suggested, but if he could just knock him out . . .

The sentry muffled a snort, and Anderson dropped, holding his breath, grinding his teeth. His heart pounded as he waited for the guard to turn around, spot him, and start the ball.

He exhaled silently. How long had he waited? A minute? Ten? His eyes found the three other men, undisturbed in their soogans, before focusing on the sentry's location. And then, above the sound of the fire, Anderson heard something that made him smile. Snoring! The guard had fallen asleep. As he crept past the tree, Anderson glanced at the man, head against his chest, revolver in its holster.

Slit his throat, Livingston had told him. *Bash in his head.* Wes decided to chance it that the guard would stay asleep. He just couldn't murder a man like this, and if he tried to knock the man out using his revolver, the chances were good that the sentry would cry out or the solid thump would awaken the others.

Looking ahead, Anderson saw the girl asleep maybe twenty yards away, and he eased toward her, occasionally glancing at the snoring man behind him and the three sleeping figures to his right, on the other side of the fire. He paused briefly, realizing that the man nearest him was an Indian whose hands were also tied.

This was unexpected, but the Indian would have to wait. First, Wesley had to get Cora Breckenridge to safety. Only after Livingston opened fire and forced the others to surrender would he help the other prisoner.

A horse neighed, and Anderson flattened as the sentry moved behind him. A few seconds passed, dragging like a long winter month, and the man mumbled something before his snoring resumed. Anderson waited for his heartbeat to slow before moving again.

It seemed like hours later, but Anderson finally found himself beside Cora. The girl's eyes darted behind her lids. Nightmare, Anderson thought, and no wonder from the looks of her face. Anger rose inside him as he opened the knife blade. A man could say some bad things about Texans, he thought, and a lot of them were gospel, but even a Texas outlaw wouldn't beat a woman.

Anderson holstered his Colt, shifted the pocketknife to his right hand, and quickly clamped his left over the girl's mouth.

Her eyes opened full of fear, and Wes grimaced as her teeth sank into his flesh, feeling her fight like a cougar under his weight. "Cora," he said in a forceful whisper, "I'm here to help." He showed her the knife, then quickly sliced the rawhide thong that bound her wrists. Next, he cut a piece of rope that secured her feet to a tree trunk.

"Who are you?" she asked as she tried to rub circulation back into her wrists and ankles.

"A friend," he said.

He slid the knife into his trousers pocket. She was looking past him now, and her eyes widened and her mouth fell open.

He moved from reflex, understanding what was happening before Cora screamed her warning. Wesley Anderson shoved the girl to the ground with his left hand and dived to his right, turning and drawing his Colt as he fell, thumbing back the hammer as a gunshot exploded and sent a bullet whipping past his ear.

Chapter Eight

*A*nderson's *luck* flashed through his mind. He should have taken Livingston's advice and killed the sentry while he slept. Wesley's left shoulder hit the ground as he fired, more from instinct than aim, at the figure behind him. The sentry was quiet—Anderson had to give him that. If it hadn't been for the girl, Wes Anderson knew he would be dead.

The man grunted after Anderson's shot, but despite being hit, he fired again. The bullet tugged at Anderson's coat collar as he rolled over and came up on his knees. The Navy Colt bucked in Anderson's hand, the sentry's hat flew from his head, and he dropped to the ground like a crashing boulder.

But Wes knew he wasn't out of this mess alive yet.

"Livingston!" he yelled as he turned to face the three remaining men. The Indian, surprisingly, remained sleeping—or at least pretending to be sleeping—on the ground, but the two other outlaws were

70

wide awake and moving. One reached for a holstered pistol hanging from a tree branch, and Anderson barely aimed and fired. The man's hand jerked back as he yelled. From the light of the campfire, Anderson saw long wood slivers stuck in the palm of the man's hand.

The other man rolled off his bedroll and lunged for a rifle, but Anderson cocked the Colt and extended his arm. "Leave it be," he said evenly. A sneer was etched in the man's ugly face, but he slowly sat up, leaving the Winchester on the ground.

Only now did the captured Indian rise to a seated position. He glanced at the dead sentry and said, "*Kap-seese*, he will sleep well tonight and forever."

It took a moment for the words to sink in. Anderson had spent two months with the Nez Percé in the early seventies, trading for the tribe's Appaloosa horses. His knowledge of the language was limited but he remembered *kap-seese*—it meant a bad person.

Wesley controlled his breathing. He shot a quick look at Cora, who pulled herself to her feet and looked around in shock, probably surprised that her ordeal was over, that she was still alive. He figured she would have run off during the shooting, and he gave her credit for staying.

The two outlaws were covered. Anderson slowly stood and surveyed the situation. Like most men, Anderson kept only five rounds in his six-shooter, a safety measure to prevent an accidental discharge. That left him only two shots until Livingston arrived. What was keeping him?

"Mind if I stand up?" one of the outlaws said. The

man rose carefully and stepped clearly into the light. Anderson froze, recognizing the face from his nightmares of the past four years and the sketches found on Wanted posters from Illinois to Oregon.

Vaughn MacDermott!

"Livingston!" Anderson yelled again.

MacDermott warmed himself at the fire, picking the splinters from his hand. "Well, son." MacDermott spoke without looking at Wes, instead concentrating on his hand, grimacing occasionally. "I'd say you've caught us fair and square, sent poor Keno to meet his maker, but what do you have in mind now?"

Anderson didn't answer. He refused to be drawn into a conversation with a snake like Major Jonathan Vaughn MacDermott. The killer would use his smooth-talk to dull Wesley's senses, charm him perhaps. And before he knew what had happened, Wes would be joining the sentry in death.

As he slowly backed his way to Keno's revolver, Anderson felt his worry grow. He had heard of MacDermott's murderous rage, had seen it firsthand on the road to Green River four years ago. It would take probably more than two shots from a .36-caliber pistol to drop either of the two outlaws, unless he hit them in the heart, so he wanted the dead man's gun as a backup. Plus, the girl was still in camp, and he worried about her. And Livingston was nowhere.

"Paul!" he called out again, then heard something behind him.

"I'm here, partner," the Mississippian's voice called out quietly from behind. Wesley sighed heavily, finally relaxing.

Livingston cocked his rifle.

Wesley felt something wrong then. Instinct or intuition, or maybe it was just the fact that he had never completely trusted Paul Livingston. He wasn't surprised or even disappointed when the former deputy added:

"Now, partner, just drop that pistol and put your hands up."

MacDermott laughed, wrapped a handkerchief around his hand, and turned to the other killer. "You see, Lane," he said, "I told you our back trail was covered."

Anderson turned and saw Livingston's rifle aimed at him. Paul nodded at Wesley's revolver, so slowly Wes let the hammer rest on the copper percussion cap as he bent his knees, placed the Colt at his feet, and straightened. He stepped back a couple of paces and raised his hands.

In the corner of his eye, he saw Cora Breckenridge sprint toward the dead sentry's gun. "No!" Wesley screamed as Livingston pivoted, the big Henry boomed and the girl fell on her back. The bullet had smashed Keno's revolver as Cora bent to pick it up, stunning her and sending her reeling to the ground.

The rifle barrel swung back to cover Anderson before he could move as Paul deftly jacked a fresh round into the chamber. Cora sat up slowly, her ears ringing, and shook her head. Anderson asked if she were all right, but Livingston replied instead, "I don't shoot women, partner."

Ignoring this, Anderson walked over and helped Cora up. She shook briefly, from rage, maybe fear, probably a combination. He asked again, quietly, if she were all right. She nodded quickly and looked up at him. "Keep your head up," he whispered to her. "We'll get out of this."

He heard the commotion behind him and turned to face his captors.

The other killer, Lane Morris, MacDermott's top hand, had whipped his bowie knife from the sheath and was making a beeline toward Anderson.

"Easy, Lane," MacDermott said, but the killer kept coming.

"He killed Keno!" Morris said and didn't stop until he heard MacDermott cock his own revolver. Morris turned to face his boss.

"Keno was going to die sooner or later. You probably would have wound up killing him yourself," MacDermott said. "Besides, this man might come in handy."

Morris swore. "There's only three of us, Major MacDermott. You, me, and Livingston. We don't need no other prisoner. That gal and Indian is more than enough."

MacDermott seemed to be considering this, so Wes looked at his Colt, calculating how far he'd need to dive to pick it up and roll over. He would die. That much was certain. He might kill one, perhaps two, but maybe during the gunfight, Cora could escape. Anderson was about to make his suicidal move when Paul Livingston spoke.

"He's an exceptional tracker," Livingston offered. "I mean he's better than any white man I've ever seen.

Plus, he's an escaped convict himself. And all he wants is part of Dunbar's gold.''

MacDermott's blue eyes bored into Anderson for a minute. ''Convict, you say.''

Livingston nodded. ''He escaped from the 'Big House' in Laramie City. And here's the poetic part: This is Wesley Anderson, Dunbar's guard that you shot. The one the judge and jury thought was riding with us and sent to prison for life.''

MacDermott's smile grew until he was laughing. He coughed, trying to suppress his cackles, and tucked his Colt .45 in his waistband. ''Well, this is a regular family reunion.''

''I still say we kill him now.'' Hate filled Lane Morris's voice.

The outlaw leader, however, shook his head. ''No, Lane, we might need a tracker before this is all over.'' Now he faced Livingston, and his words came out with force. ''But he's your responsibility, Paul. And if he tries anything, he's dead.''

Livingston nodded, and he looked at Anderson. The Mississippian's eyes seemed to be saying, *I just saved your life again, partner. Now don't mess it up.* Wes considered this for a second, then heard Morris swearing.

The killer angrily threw his knife into the dirt and looked at Anderson's Colt on the ground nearby. He picked it up, walked to Anderson, and smiled. ''I guess it can wait,'' he said, and slammed the butt of the revolver across Anderson's head.

Anderson dropped to his knees. A parade of colors

passed by, then he was swallowed up by a sea of darkness.

June 1873

Wes Anderson looked at the blue roan horse writhing on the ground, its front right leg shattered. Frowning, Wes placed the Colt's muzzle against the animal's head and fired. After stripping off the saddle and bridle, Anderson began the two-hour hike to the Dunbar Mine Road. *Anderson's luck*, he thought as he stopped to wipe his sweaty forehead.

Hoofbeats sounded, and Wesley dropped his tack and waited. Four riders crested the hill. One man called out an order, and a black wagon reined to a stop on the road, quickly flanked by other riders. Twelve men rode as outriders, and another three sat perched on the hearse. Every one of them carried a Winchester '66 carbine and handgun; some carried two revolvers. About half a dozen rifles were now trained on Anderson.

Anderson waited as one rider eased his black mare toward him. The man had reddish brown hair and a handlebar mustache, and kept his rifle cradled across his lap so that when he finally stopped, the barrel pointed at Wesley's chest.

"What are you doin' here?" the man asked. There was no malice in his voice, and little curiosity.

"Lost my horse," Anderson answered. "I was hoping to see Mr. Dunbar about a job."

The rider's gray eyes considered the Navy Colt in Anderson's holster. "You any good with that thing?" he asked.

Wesley shrugged. "I hit what I aim," he said, then added so it wouldn't sound like a brag, "usually."

"What makes you think that Mr. Dunbar is hirin'?"

"Word in South Pass City is that he's taking a shipment to the railroad in Green River," he answered. "That he needs some guards."

The rider shook his head. "So much for secrets, eh?" He jerked a thumb toward the hilltop, where the others waited, and Wesley walked ahead, leaving the saddle and bridle on the roadside because he didn't feel like lugging them with him. The man on horseback followed and when Wesley stood in front of the hearse, the man yelled: "Mr. Dunbar?"

The back door to the hearse opened, and a rail-thin, gray-haired man with bushy eyebrows and a thick mustache stepped out. He wore canvas trousers and a plaid shirt, no hat and no gun. Alec Dunbar certainly didn't look like the richest man in the South Pass district.

"Aye," Dunbar said as his blue eyes found Wesley. "What can I do for ye, lad?"

The rider answered. "He says he lost his horse a ways back, says he was ridin' out to find you and wants a job as a guard. And he says all of South Pass City knows your plans to haul the shipment to the railroad."

"Aye. Is that so, Gregory? But I was asking the lad."

"It's true," Wes said. "I'd like to join you, if you'll have me."

"Dangerous work," the Scotsman said.

"I need the job," Wes answered. He didn't want to

tell Dunbar that he hadn't eaten in two days, that the only person hiring in the district was Alec Dunbar. Everybody else seemed to be feeling the pinch of poverty. Wes doubted if he could have found work emptying spittoons in a South Pass saloon.

Dunbar jutted his long jaw at Anderson's waist. "Let's see how well you handle that Navy .36, young man," Dunbar said, and he fished a silver dollar from his trousers pocket and flipped it across the road, high in the air.

Anderson's motions were slow, it seemed. Three fingers slipped around the Colt's walnut butt while his index finger found the brass trigger guard and his thumb pressed back the case-hardened hammer. He heard the distinct metallic clicks as the hammer fell to full cock, rotating the engraved cylinder. The .36 already stretched out from the end of his right arm, and Wesley found the spinning piece of silver against the blue sky. He notched the brass bead at the end of the shiny black barrel between the narrow slit on the hammer, led the coin a ways, and pulled the trigger.

A horse snorted. Wesley's eyes burned from the thick, acrid smoke, but he stepped upwind, thumbed back the hammer, and saw the coin spinning higher, rapidly shooting across the sky. His Colt barked again, and this time he saw the coin cut sharply to the left and plunge to the ground.

There was no way he could hit it again, so he sought out a rock, cocked the Colt and aimed briefly, but stopped. He had hit the dollar twice, had proved his point. To shoot again would be nothing more than showing off, maybe even begging for a job.

He squeezed the trigger, releasing the hammer, which he lowered slowly with his thumb until the hammer set safely against a fresh percussion cap. Anderson turned to face Alec Dunbar and slid the Navy Colt into its holster.

The Scotsman smiled. "Laddie, this looks like a lucky day for you, and for me."

Chapter Nine

September 1877

He came to with a start, squinting in the morning sunlight, and felt something cold against his pounding head as his vision cleared, the nightmare faded, and he saw Cora beside him, wiping the purple knot above his temple with a wet bandanna. Her smile seemed obviously forced, and maybe Anderson would have returned it, but his ears rang and blood hammered against his skull.

"Who are you?" Cora asked.

Wesley took the compress from her hands and squeezed it against his head. He smelled coffee and bacon but wasn't sure he could keep anything in his stomach. Not after Morris had almost cracked his head open. Cora repeated her question, and Wesley let the rag fall to the ground as he filled his lungs with cold, morning air.

He fought off a wave of nausea and told her, "Wesley Anderson."

"That was not my meaning."

"I know," he said weakly, and rested his aching head in his cupped hands.

"Is it true?" she asked. "What they say? That you escaped from the territorial prison?"

He sighed. "Yes," he said, and she drew away. He reached for her, not wanting her to be afraid of him, not wanting her to be repulsed by him. He needed her if they were to escape, and she needed him. She had to trust him. His right hand caught her fingers and gave them a gentle squeeze.

"Cora," he said, "I'm no outlaw. Last night, Paul Livingston told MacDermott that I'm the one the jury *thought* was with them. Remember?" Her head bobbed slightly. "I'm not one of them." He nodded at the killers, who hungrily ate their breakfast while the Indian sat silently beside them, smoking one of MacDermott's cigarettes.

"I know every man who goes into the 'Big House' probably says the same thing, but I was innocent," Wesley pleaded. He thought about his nightmare, shook his head, and told her what had happened on the road more than four summers ago.

June 1873

Alec Dunbar nodded with satisfaction at Wesley's marksmanship, and the rider named Gregory commented, "We could use him on the hearse, Mr. Dunbar, what with us bein' a man down because Roberts got sick."

The Scotsman agreed and led Anderson to the hearse. He opened one of the strongboxes and produced a leather pouch, sprinkling some of the sparkling nuggets in his hands before returning it. Anderson couldn't help but stare at the pouches, each burned with the initials A.D.

"A pouch for every guard," Dunbar said, "once we reach the railroad. Are these terms acceptable?"

Wes could only nod. He was thunderstruck by the sight of that much gold. There were fifteen guards, not including Dunbar or himself, and Wesley guessed that each pouch was probably worth at least twelve hundred dollars. The hearse was so heavy with treasure that its wheels sank into the dirt, and the muscular horses already showed the sign of strain. Anderson and Dunbar shook hands, and Wesley climbed onto the top of the hearse, sliding in beside the gray-bearded driver. The man whipped the reins, and the party resumed the journey while Anderson dropped into the boot to block the wind and reloaded his Colt.

Dunbar and his men bypassed South Pass, traveling on the high road east. This certainly would be the long way to reach Green River, but Wes understood it might be safer. He knew they had been mistaken when the riders were forced to stop high atop a hill several miles east of Atlantic City.

A fallen tree blocked the narrow road.

But no trees grew on the hill.

The driver set the brake, while a couple of outriders dismounted and roped the downed aspen. Wesley looked north at the flat valley that stretched toward the Wind River country, then studied the countryside at the bottom of the hill to the south. A creek wound its way into the forest, and Wes spotted a beaver dam.

He saw where an ax had chopped the tree below, saw the markings on the grass where a couple of horses had dragged the timber from the valley near the creek uphill and left it blocking the road.

Anderson swore and looked around for some sign of an ambush. He dropped to the ground and yelled, "It's a trap!" He still hadn't seen anyone but hoped his cry would cause the ambushers—wherever they were—to panic.

It worked. A shot rang out from the beaver dam and lodged in the side of the hearse. "The dam!" Anderson yelled, and Gregory dismounted and opened fire on the dam with his Winchester. Two other riders joined him. Another rifle cracked from the timbers, but by now Dunbar's riders were ready.

The attackers were out of range for the Navy. He wished he had a long gun as he moved his way to the rear of the hearse. A rider jacked a shell into the Winchester and snapped off a quick shot at Anderson, drilling a hole through Wesley's hat and clipping a few hairs.

He realized what was happening and flattened himself underneath the wagon, aimed, and shot the rider off his horse. Some of Dunbar's men had helped set up the ambush. He heard horses pounding up the hill as he rolled underneath the wagon and came up on the opposite side on his knees. A bullet ricocheted off a rock by his feet, and Wesley shot another man. Then he pulled himself up and slapped the side of the hearse.

"Mr. Dunbar!" he yelled. "We've got to get out of here!"

The gray-haired driver saw Wesley and brought up an old Dance .44 and sent a bullet grazing Anderson's cheek. *Another traitor*, Wes thought, but before he could return fire, the driver groaned suddenly, burying his hands into his thick gut, and pitched forward, landing at Wesley's boots. Wes saw Gregory climbing into the driver's boot, lowering his smoking rifle as he desperately tried to release the brake.

Gregory's body jerked twice and fell heavily on the top of the wagon. A bullet whined past Anderson's ear. He shoved the Colt into his holster and pulled himself into the driver's boot. A quick look at Gregory told him the man was dead. About that time, the riders crested the hill.

The Colt came into Wesley's hand and he fired at the closest newcomer, thumbed back the hammer and made sure of his target. A black-bearded rider spun from his saddle, and Wesley reached for Gregory's Winchester.

He saw the outlaw then, clearly, a blue-eyed, blond-haired man with a well-groomed mustache and tailor-made clothes. Wes lifted the rifle, slamming in a fresh round as the man whipped a nickel-plated revolver from a red sash and fired.

Anderson felt himself flying off the wagon. He hit the ground hard, and air shot from his lungs as his feet kicked awkwardly. His left shoulder was numb, and suddenly he was rolling over and over down the gentle hill, rapidly accelerating, until his body skimmed across the creek and came to a rest against the beaver dam.

Wesley hugged the wood for a minute, fighting off dizziness and sickness, and moved slowly to the bank, forgetting that several outlaws were hidden behind the dam and in the trees. And apparently the attackers forgot about Anderson. Or maybe they couldn't see him, focusing their attack on the riders on top of the hill. Somehow, he reached the solid ground. He felt the pain then as he sank to his knees and brought his right hand against his shoulder, sticky with warm blood. The gunshots seemed far away now. His chest heaved, and he sank wearily to the ground.

Blood and strength drained out of him, and he tried to swallow, yet couldn't. The sounds of the gunshots died and he heard footsteps and shouts, but his head was too heavy to raise. Heavy eyelids closed. When they opened, it was dusk.

A fuzzy figure finally came into focus, and Anderson stared down the barrel of a miner's musket. The man was bearded and toothless, and his blue eyes held no mercy. "You murdering little thief," the miner growled, cocking the hammer.

"Leave him be!" someone shouted.

"What for?"

"Because, you dumb oaf. He might tell us where the gold is!"

September 1877

So they hauled him back to South Pass City and threw him in the jail, finally letting a doctor see him after two days. Wes told Cora about the near-lynching, about the speedy trial and about his journey to the new penitentiary in Laramie. He skipped the details of his four years of wrongful imprisonment and simply told her how he had escaped, how he had met her father in the saloon, then found his body in the South Pass Livery.

She cast her eyes down. Wes paused. "I'm sorry," he said after a minute.

Cora shook her head. "It's—" She stopped and looked up, quickly wiping her cheeks and letting out a soft laugh. "Was he happy—when he came into the saloon?"

"Yeah," Wes replied with a smile. "He was definitely happy. The bartender told him he should get back to you, but he said you could take care of yourself. I think he said something about howling at the moon when he left Fort Bourbon."

Cora nodded. "He said that all the time. And when he was in his cups, he would howl at the moon. I mean he sounded just like a wolf—a wolf that has had his watering hole spiked with rye whiskey."

They both laughed. It felt good, Wesley thought, trying to remember the last time he had laughed.

Vaughn MacDermott cleared his throat. The smiles left Cora and Wes instantly as they looked up at the killer. MacDermott knelt beside them. At the edge of camp, Livingston and Morris saddled the horses while Hohops rolled another cigarette. Anderson focused on MacDermott's face. The mustache was gone, but the blue eyes were the same—cold, icy, unfeeling. He could see the man again, sitting on a prancing black stallion and firing a fancy revolver.

Wesley brought up his fingers and rubbed the scar on his shoulder, left by Vaughn MacDermott's bullet and a drunken doctor's scalpel.

"Ugly bump," MacDermott said, staring at the knot on Anderson's head.

"I'll live" was Wesley's reply.

"Well, we'll see about that." Then he made his pitch. "All we want is the gold. No one has to be hurt. No one has to die. We find the gold, you get a share, the girl gets a share, and we go our separate ways."

"Do I get my Colt back?" Anderson asked.

MacDermott laughed. "No, then Lane might have a reason to kill you. I sometimes have a hard time keeping Lane Morris reined in. I probably should just kill him myself and find somebody new, but, well, Lane's been with me for fifteen years, and I do have a sentimental side."

"And Livingston?" Anderson asked. "Where does he fit in?"

"Paul was with Lee Thorn in the trees when we hit you and Dunbar. I found Paul in Bannack City back in '68 or '69. We went our separate ways after the Dunbar tragedy, and a few years back he got hired as a deputy in South Pass. So we decided to stay in touch. We've all been watching that old miner Breckenridge and his lovely daughter." He cast a quick glance at Cora. "He was always looking for the gold, so it kind of saved us a lot of time and effort."

MacDermott stood. "We won't tie you up unless you try something stupid. Remember, Anderson, that you want some of that gold. And I for one believe you deserve a cut. Four years in that dungeon." Mac-

Dermott shook his head. "Help us out, and I'll see that you get a fair share. Let's get ready to move."

Cora helped Anderson to his feet. He gingerly touched his head, then moved toward his horse, slowly looking around the camp. Keno lay were he had fallen, spread-eagled on the ground.

"What about him?" Anderson asked. "We should bury him."

"Nah," MacDermott said. "Waste of time. Besides, we'll just leave him here and when some prospector comes up and finds his bones, he'll just chalk it up to the curse of Dunbar's gold."

Chapter Ten

The day passed quickly. The Popo Agie River churned angrily past sandstone cliffs, splitting a world of pine trees and junipers and sagebrush. It was here that MacDermott pitched camp before dusk. Wesley Anderson stumbled through the brambles and knelt on a dark granite boulder, where cascading white water splashed his face and shirt and quickly cooled him, dulling his headache at last. He wet his hands and ran his fingers through knotted hair, worked his lungs— and memorized the country.

Cora sat beside him, cupping her hands and drinking thirstily. MacDermott had not let them eat all day, and had allowed only a few sips of water during their forced march. "Just like a cattle drive," the major had said. "You push the cows hard the first couple of days from home so they're less likely to stampede."

The girl glared at him. "What do you know about

89

cattle drives?'' she asked bitingly. ''That's honest work.''

Wesley had smiled at that, though he wondered how MacDermott would respond. The killer merely laughed, however, and quipped, ''Well, ma'am, I've rustled a few cows in my career.''

Anderson balled up his wet bandanna and pressed it against his head. The knot where Morris had bludgeoned him was shrinking. He looked past Cora. Paul Livingston stood fifteen yards away, resting the barrel of his nickel-plated rifle on his shoulder. Beyond Paul, Lane Morris tethered and hobbled the mules and horses while MacDermott broke out the grub and Hohops gathered firewood.

''Cora,'' Wesley said, and the girl looked at him.

The roar of the river, echoing off the massive cliffs, would drown out their conversation, Anderson thought. Even Livingston couldn't hear them.

''Can you swim?''

She nodded, but considered the river uncertainly.

''The rapids aren't as hard about a hundred yards upstream,'' he said, nodding in the direction. ''They're still dangerous, but there's a pool.'' He stood up and offered her his hand, pulling Cora to her feet and jutting his chin upstream.

Cora saw the pool, where an uprooted pine stretched halfway across the Popo Agie. She understood. They could crawl over the tree as far as they could, drop into the water, and swim hard for the opposite bank. With luck, they would reach the shore just before the current's intensity became too strong to fight.

''When?'' she whispered.

"They'll turn in early. They pushed themselves hard today too. When they're all asleep, I'll get you. If they post a guard and he doesn't fall asleep, though, don't try anything. We'll find another chance later."

Cora nodded.

"That's enough talking, friends!" Livingston shouted, swinging his rifle around for added punctuation. "Get on back up here!"

Wes sat up slowly, listening to the steady, deep breathing of the three outlaws. Satisfied, Anderson rolled off his bedroll and crawled toward the fire. Morris had tied Wesley's hands before turning in, so Anderson pulled a piece of wood from the edge of the fire and held the rope over the burning end. He ignored the burning sensation in his palms, biting his lip, and finally pulled the charred rope apart.

MacDermott, Livingston, and Morris still slept. He thought of the Indian prisoner, but when Anderson turned to find the Nez Percé holy man, he couldn't.

Hohops had disappeared.

Anderson's head shot back and forth, but he found no signs of the Indian, and he couldn't waste any time searching for the man. The gray sky was growing lighter in the east, and Wesley didn't have much time to grab Cora, swim the river, and find a safe hiding place in the forest. Morris, the last man on guard duty, had taken a long time before he fell asleep.

Anderson thought briefly about making for one of the guns but ruled against it. Too risky. Not enough time. Instead, he inched his way to Cora, who was already awake. Using the ragged edge of a stone, she had sawed through the rawhide thong Livingston had wrapped around her hands. But she had listened to Anderson and waited for him.

"You seen Hohops?" Wesley whispered.

Cora shook her head.

"He must have taken off during the night, but I didn't hear him. Let's get out of here."

They crawled to the edge of camp. A horse snorted, causing them to pause. The two waited a couple of minutes before continuing on hands and knees for ten more yards, then climbing to their feet and running softly to the bank of the Popo Agie, letting the sound of the river muffle their footsteps.

The sky turned lighter, and a misty steam rose from the pool. Cora scrambled up the fallen pine and hurried to the end. Anderson followed but stopped halfway and waited on the girl. He wasn't sure the tree would support their weight, so he would let Cora dive in first. He hoped she wasn't lying to him, that she could indeed swim.

"Hurry," he whispered. Cora was at the end now, but she hesitated, glancing downstream where the current and rocks turned the water into a frothing, churning menace.

A rifle cracked, and the bullet tore off a chunk of bark inches from Wesley's right hand. In the dim light, he looked down the bank, saw Paul Livingston jack another round into his Henry rifle. Livingston called out something, but Anderson couldn't hear him over the rapids.

Wesley heard the splash, and saw that Cora had

dropped into the river. Her head shot up and she spit out water, splashing frantically as the current pulled her under and downstream. The river was stronger here than he had expected. Wesley heard another bullet whine over his head. This time he could understand Livingston's words:

"Stop, Wesley! Don't make me kill you!"

Behind Paul, MacDermott and Morris came running. Wes turned back at Cora, saw her struggling desperately, and he dived into the river.

The freezing water made him gasp for air. He swallowed a mouthful of water and pulled himself to the surface, kicked his legs, and swam fast for Cora. She sank again, came up, and screamed for help.

Wesley reached her, locked his right hand around a wrist, and pulled. She twisted against him, and they sank, hit the bottom, and bounced up. Cora tried to climb on top of him. He yelled something, but couldn't understand his own words because of the deafening sound of the river. He looked up, felt the current sweeping harder, realized they were closer to the first fall than he realized.

"Cora!" he yelled, and gasped for breath. She mumbled something.

A movement caught his eye on the far bank. He realized it was Hohops, running out of the juniper thicket, crawling over a gray boulder and reaching his bony hands toward them. Wesley planted his feet on the rocky bottom and shoved, practically threw, Cora to the Nez Percé. She splashed near the boulder, yelled, and then Hohops had a handful of her hair with his right hand, and quickly locked his left around her arm.

Hohops let go of her hair, gripped her right hand and arm with his, and pulled her up the rocks to safety. By then, the Popo Agie had swept Anderson off his feet and hurled him over the first small waterfall.

He crashed against a rock, tried to breathe but could find no oxygen, felt his descent increase as his body was slammed against a jagged rock, which the current pushed him over and drove him through a narrow slice between two giant gray stones. Anderson planted his feet downstream, forced his eyes open, and looked for help, something he could latch on to, but he was moving too fast, and the sound of the rapids became even louder. He was close to the shore. He could feel it, but couldn't stop himself. Another boulder rapidly approached him. Wesley bent his knees and felt the jarring collision as his boots slammed into the rock. His legs folded and then he kicked himself away from the boulder, landed with a thud in shallow water, and sought out help with his hands, splashing, bouncing like a landed trout as the current tried to pull him to his death.

His hands gripped something narrow and cold. At first he thought he had found a branch, but he felt himself being pulled from the river. He was out of the water now, shivering from the cold, spitting up water, coughing, heaving. His ribs ached with each breath, and he wondered if he had cracked them on the rock.

Anderson wiped his brow and looked up. Paul Livingston sat on the bank, breathing rapidly, holding the Henry unsteadily.

Realization came slow to Wesley, but he soon understood that he had not grasped a branch. His hands had gripped the rifle barrel, and Livingston had pulled him out of the Popo Agie.

"I'd . . . say . . . that   I   saved . . . your   life . . . again," Livingston choked out.

Hohops and Cora were shoved forward by MacDermott and Morris. The major tossed a waterlogged hat into Wesley's lap, while Cora sank to her knees and rubbed her pale arms rapidly, trying to warm herself. Morris glared at Anderson and said dryly, "We ought to kill him now. Be done with him."

MacDermott shook his head. "Not yet. But from now on, we chain them to a tree when we turn in."

"I still say—"

"I ought to kill *you!*" MacDermott shouted savagely. "You were the one who fell asleep on guard duty, Lane. Now let's get moving."

Wesley nodded at Cora. "She needs time by a fire, some dry clothes."

MacDermott shook his head. "Sun will be up soon. She can warm up then."

They were in the Wind River mountain range when they made camp. Wesley stripped off his shirt and looked at his side. A dark bruise, bookended by two long cuts, had formed over his rib cage. He touched the wound hesitantly, then pressed his hand harder with a grimace. The ribs weren't broken after all, but they sure hurt like blazes.

His wrists hurt as well. MacDermott had made sure Cora and Anderson were securely bounded to their saddle horns, and for good measure had tied their legs with a small piece of rope stretching under the belly of their horses. Hohops rode an Army horse, and since the McClellan saddle had no horn, Morris tied a rope around the skinny Indian's waist and wrapped it around his own saddle horn.

Anderson flexed his wrists to get the blood circulating again. His thighs were chafed from the saddle, his feet raw from the wet boots, and his stomach ached for meat and water. This, he thought, was worse than prison.

"Mr. Anderson?"

Wes saw Cora standing by him and quickly pulled on his ragged shirt. His face warmed, and he knew he was blushing.

Cora smiled at his modesty. Anderson finally laughed slightly himself, regretting the slight jarring of his ribs.

"Call me Wesley, or Wes," he said, and motioned her to sit beside him.

"I'm sorry about this morning," she said. "I mean, I almost drowned you."

"Forget it."

"But I lied to you. I can't swim. I should have told you that before, but I thought you'd leave me."

He grabbed the fingers on her right hand and squeezed them slightly. "I'm not going to leave you, Cora," he said. "I'll get you out of here. Then I'll take care of MacDermott. After that, maybe we can find Dunbar's gold ourselves."

She pulled away from him.

"You want the gold?" she asked incredulously.

"Yes, ma'am," he said.

"Why?"

He had to refrain from laughing. "It's worth one hundred thousand dollars, Cora. Maybe more. And I think Wyoming owes me that after the four years I spent in prison."

Cora sat up and walked away. Anderson ran his fingers through his hair, a movement that also hurt his ribs, and he wondered what he had said, why the Breckenridge girl suddenly acted so strangely.

"I feel sorry for you, Mr. Anderson," she said, and headed for the fire Hohops had built.

Chapter Eleven

"Which way?" MacDermott's voice was a growl.

Cora shook her head. "I haven't been up here in years. This country looks the same. This could be the trail, or it might lead to nowhere. I'm just not sure."

Lane Morris swore.

MacDermott pushed back his hat and rubbed both temples as he considered the fork in the trail. Wearily he turned to Hohops and asked the Indian the same question. The Nez Percé *tewat* smiled and shrugged.

"As you have mentioned before, this is not the land of my people."

"But you said you've seen the gold. You—"

"I have seen the gold. It waits for you in the cave high in these mountains. But I have seen this only in my vision."

"A vision!" MacDermott palmed one of his Colt

revolvers and thumbed back the hammer, aiming the barrel at the medicine man's forehead. "I ought to kill you right now. A vision!" He cursed angrily.

A movement caught MacDermott's eyes, and he swung around in the saddle as Anderson dismounted and walked forward a few steps, knelt, and placed his bounded hands on the dirt. "Paul," MacDermott said, "I told you to tie him to the saddle horn. Anderson, get your carcass back in that saddle or I'll blow your head off."

Anderson looked MacDermott in the eye and nodded at the trail that veered to the left. "It's this way," Wes said mildly and pointed at the dirt. Livingston swung off his horse and studied the markings in the ground.

"It's a shod horse, Vaughn," Paul said excitedly. "But the sign must be old."

"Several weeks," Wes agreed. "And it's from a mule, coming down the mountains. Breckenridge's mule."

MacDermott lowered his revolver. "How can you tell?"

"The markings are the same," Anderson answered. "It's from the mule's left rear shoe. We have the mule. You can compare the tracks yourself if you want."

The Colt clicked softly as MacDermott carefully lowered the hammer and slid the revolver into his sash. "Well," he said, "since Miss Cora and Mr. Hohops aren't much good to us now, lead the way, Mr. Anderson."

Anderson held up his hands. "Cut these free," he said.

The major frowned.

"I'll have to climb on and off my horse, study the ground carefully. Following a trail this old is hard enough without having rawhide biting my wrists."

MacDermott clucked his tongue for a second before nodding slightly. Livingston pulled out Anderson's pocketknife, opened the blade and cut the leather thong. Wesley rubbed his wrists awhile before gathering the reins to his horse and walking up the narrow trail.

"And, Anderson," MacDermott said, "if you try anything stupid, the first person to die will be the girl."

The climb grew tougher on men and animals and the wind harsher as they moved past the boulders toward Gunsight Pass. When they were forced to dismount and walk the horses, Anderson wondered how Breckenridge had been able to travel up the steep grade with a mule.

Anderson was at the point, scouting several yards ahead of the others. He—and MacDermott—knew he couldn't escape, couldn't leave Cora behind with the killers. So he concentrated on the trail, and the fortune in gold. Something glinted in the dimming sunlight near the rocks at the base of a barren ridge and he eased toward it, then grimaced and waited for the others.

It was a lonely place to die, he thought, as he stared at the skeleton of a prospector. Many of the bones had been scattered over time, but the rib cage remained intact. And although the handle had rotted away, a rusty pickax was still stuck in the man's chest.

"Nasty way to die," said Livingston, the first to arrive.

"Murdered," Anderson said.

"Yup. I reckon that old Breckenridge didn't enjoy company. Or maybe it was the ghost." He laughed, and Anderson tugged at the reins of the horse and moved on. Anderson knew Horace Breckenridge wasn't the type to murder a man with a pickax. And Wes didn't believe in ghosts.

Slowly the procession moved past the remains, each glancing silently at the miner, keeping their thoughts to themselves as the evening wind howled what seemed to be a warning.

Anderson blew into the cup of steaming coffee and watched as Hohops used a twig from the fire to light a cigarette. Wes put the coffee aside to let it cool and said, "I haven't thanked you for helping pull Cora out of the river."

The Indian smiled. "You have no reason to thank me. Nor does the girl."

"You saved her life."

"No. I stopped you two from escaping."

The bewildered expression on Wesley's face amused Hohops. He took a long drag on the cigarette and exhaled, watching the white smoke drift toward the trees. With his left hand, he scooped up dirt from the ground and tossed it between Anderson's boots.

"Mother Earth told me that you would try to escape, try to ford the river, so I left before you. I knew you would fail, but the girl must not die. I threw a rock across the river that awakened the man called Livingston, and you know the rest.''

''Why would you do that? You're a prisoner too.''

''I would like to see the Lair Which Weeps. But if the girl is harmed, the spirits will be angry.''

Hohops pulled hard on the cigarette and rose. ''You will need a friend to survive this journey, Anderson, but I am not that person.''

The medicine man turned and left, leaving Wesley staring blankly into the small fire. Anderson had no idea how long he sat like that. Scattered thoughts shot through his mind. He heard a throat being cleared and looked up to see Cora sitting where Hohops had been.

''Your coffee's getting cold,'' she said. There was no humor in her voice.

He sipped the brew. He had tasted better swill in prison. Cora stared at the flames. Neither felt like talking, so Wesley pulled the pennywhistle from his boot. He went through the range of notes, started one song but decided against it and settled on ''Lorena.'' In the ''Big House,'' he could play that love song so well he'd have his cellmates and even an occasional guard wiping his eyes.

Once, a husky Welsh convict serving twenty years for robbery cleared his throat and joined in with a beautiful baritone:

> *I hardly feel the cold, Lorena,*
> *Soon this darkness too shall pass.*

We'll sing those songs again, Lorena,
You'll be in my arms at last.

He concentrated on the notes, trying to block out the reality of his desperate situation, but couldn't. He missed a few notes, rare for him, but his audience didn't notice. MacDermott cleaned his Colt revolvers, Morris sharpened his knife, and Livingston stood by the animals talking to Hohops. The only person paying attention was Cora, who looked up when he had finished and smiled.

"That was beautiful," she said.

"Thanks."

"How did you learn to play?"

"I taught myself," he said, leaving out the fact that he had learned in prison.

She started to laugh but stopped herself. "Pa used to say he'd buy me a big old grand piano when he struck it rich, set it up in the parlor, and have me play 'From Greenland's Icy Mountains' over and over again."

"I don't know that one," Wes said.

"Good," she said, and they both smiled.

"Do you . . ." She paused, the smile disappearing, and continued, "Do you think MacDermott's telling the truth, that he'll let us go?"

He saw the concern on her face and tried to sound reassuring. "No reason not to," he lied. "We might not get an even split, but I don't think he'll kill us. There's enough gold to go around."

Anger flared in her eyes and she said in a sharp whisper, "You don't have to lie to me. He had his own men ambush his partner—my father told me all about that—for this gold years ago. There wasn't enough to go around then; there still isn't.''

Silence hovered over them for several seconds. *Then why did you ask me in the first place?* Wesley thought to himself, but he kept quiet. Cora finally mumbled an apology. She stared at the ground for a moment, looked at Anderson again, and spoke, struggling with the words.

''We . . . we don't see things . . . eye to eye. I . . . I don't want anything to do with Dunbar's gold. You want it. But . . . I don't want to die up here, alone.''

He reached out and started to pull her close, but he stopped, uncertain how she would react. Cora Breckenridge was independent, a good woman, strong, but not as tough as she pretended to be. Wesley Anderson was a saddle tramp, gunman, escaped convict. He had no business even looking at a woman like Cora. Why would she ever have anything to do with the likes of him?

''Cora,'' he said. ''I'm not some hardened killer. I promise you that I won't risk your life for the gold.''

She nodded. ''Tell me about Pa,'' she said. ''When you found him in the livery. Did . . . was . . . did he suffer?''

The vision of Horace Breckenridge in the stall returned and Anderson swallowed hard. ''They hit him some, but when they killed him, I'm sure he felt no pain.'' It was a lie, a bad lie, because Breckenridge had died in agony, bleeding to death, trying to hold his guts inside. Anderson fought back nausea just thinking about it.

Cora knew he was lying again, but this time she smiled. "Thanks for lying, Wesley, but you don't have to."

"Yeah," he said, sighing. "Well, death never comes easy, be it by bullet, knife, or natural causes. At least, that's how I see it."

She was crying then, and angry about it. Anderson rose and put his hand on her arm. She tightened for a second. "It's all right, Cora," he said softly. "Let the pain run its course."

He felt her relax, and he pulled her close. "I'll be your friend, Cora. I'm here for you." Her head rested on his shoulder and she sobbed silently. He stroked her hair, but his movements were awkward, uneven. At first, he wasn't sure what he was supposed to do. But Anderson remembered comforting his mother and sister during the late War after receiving word of his father's death, then again after his brother was killed. He felt Cora's pain.

"Well, well, well," Morris said callously, and Cora straightened, turning to face the killer. Morris hovered over them and spit a stream of tobacco juice into the fire.

"Ain't this sweet. Perfect Wesley Anderson comforting the little girl, taking care of her like the gentleman he is. Gentleman, hah. Convict."

Cora Breckenridge stood quickly, and a swift kick into Morris's kneecap let him know she could take care of herself when she had to. Morris fell to his side and exploded with anger as MacDermott and Livingston—even Hohops—laughed.

Morris opened fire with an assault of venomous profanity. He furiously pulled Anderson's Navy Colt from his waistband and was starting to cock it when Anderson kicked the gun from his hand. "Get back, Cora," Wesley said, dropping into a boxer's stance.

Lane Morris grinned without humor. This was what he wanted: a chance to tear Wesley Anderson to pieces, to rip him apart as he had the miner back in that South Pass City livery. Livingston and Mac-Dermott made bets on the fight and moved toward the fire. Cora tried to step between Morris and Anderson, but Hohops's bony fingers gripped her wrists and yanked her away, pulling her behind MacDermott and Livingston.

"Lane," MacDermott said sternly.

"We should have killed him days ago!" Morris shouted.

"We need him alive, Lane," Paul said. "You want to fight him, fight him. But use your fists."

Morris cursed again before slowly unbuckling his gun belt. He tossed it toward the Navy Colt on the ground nearby, but at the last second jerked the big bowie knife from its sheath.

Chapter Twelve

Anderson had expected this. Lane Morris wouldn't dare fight him with just his fists. Wesley sucked in his gut and jumped back as the knife slashed a deadly path through the air. Livingston said something, and MacDermott mumbled a reply, but Anderson couldn't understand the words, and neither man did anything to stop Morris. Wes dodged another slice from the bowie. He was on the defensive, backing up quickly as Morris lashed out with the big knife, as if he were some Eastern-factory machine.

The killer paused to get a better grip and smiled at Anderson, who took advantage of the break to catch his breath.

"Stop him!" Cora yelled at MacDermott and Livingston as she fought Hohops's grip. "He'll kill him. Stop him!"

"Not yet," MacDermott said. "I've got money on Lane."

Wesley quickly glanced at MacDermott and Livingston. Paul stood cold-faced, both fists clenched, eyes hard. He actually looked worried. To MacDermott, however, the fight was a game. He didn't care whether Anderson died, and probably wouldn't mind if he killed Morris. "Come on, sonny, quit running and fight the man!" MacDermott said, laughing.

But Anderson saw nothing funny. Morris moved forward. Wes leaped away from the blade, watching Morris skillfully move the knife from one hand to the other, then slash out again, barely missing him. The blade came back, and Anderson heard his coat rip. Both men were gasping in the thin air, and suddenly Morris grunted as the knife swished past and the momentum carried him to the ground.

Anderson quickly shed his coat—it was slowing him down—and kicked out toward the fallen killer, but his boot just missed Morris's chin and while he was recovering his balance, Morris was back on his feet, coming at him like an animal, grunting with every thrust of the blade.

The bowie ripped Anderson's shirt, and he felt something sticky running down his stomach. Morris grinned, but Anderson knew it was only a scratch. The blade attacked again, ripping a button off his shirt. Wesley was slowing. He knew he couldn't go on like this, backing up, dodging, always on the defensive. He needed to fight back, to move to the offensive, to catch Morris off-guard.

Suddenly Morris lunged at him, yelling like a charging Confederate soldier, bringing the blade arcing up toward Anderson's chest.

A quick pivot saved Anderson's life and changed the direction of the fight. As Morris lunged past him, Anderson grabbed a handful of the killer's hair with his left hand and clamped his right hand on Morris's right wrist, holding the knife, and he pushed Morris, the momentum carrying both men forward into a tree.

They grunted on impact. Anderson forced the bowie's blade deep into the pine. At the same time he yanked Morris's head back and slammed his face into the trunk. The killer groaned as blood poured from his nose. Anderson released the man's wrist with his right hand and gave Morris a savage kidney punch.

He didn't let up, though his chest heaved and he felt weak. Wes pulled Morris around to face him, slammed the back of his head against the tree, and sent a crashing right into his jaw that dropped Morris to the ground. The killer made a weak effort to rise, then fell still.

Gasping for air, Wes Anderson moved away from Morris a few yards, leaned against a tree and slowly slid into a sitting position. Cora was beside him, ripping off part of her blouse to use as a bandage on the cut across his stomach.

Vaughn MacDermott frowned, silently pulled a gold coin from his coat pocket, and handed it to a smiling Livingston. Hohops simply shrugged, squatted, and began feeding the fire with fresh wood. The major and Livingston walked to Morris's crumpled body. MacDermott kicked him over. When the man didn't budge, Livingston knelt.

"Out cold," he said finally, "and he'll want to kill the both of them when he comes to."

"It's his fault we're in this fix," MacDermott said. "If he hadn't killed the old miner in the livery . . ."

MacDermott stared at Anderson, still gasping for air while the girl doctored his knife wound. Livingston looked up, first at his boss, then at his "partner." He knew what MacDermott was thinking. They needed the girl, if only to point out the pass and find her father's camp, but Anderson was expendable. And after seeing him manhandle a seasoned killer like Morris, MacDermott no doubt felt he was more trouble than he was worth. Anderson had already tried to escape once, and his skill with a six-gun was undeniable.

Paul Livingston was fond of Wesley Anderson and his pennywhistle for various reasons, one of them quite selfish: Livingston didn't trust Major Vaughn MacDermott, and if he kept Anderson alive he might have an extra gun hand to go against MacDermott— if needed.

"The kid's a better tracker than any of us," Livingston said. "And we might need that before we're done."

MacDermott grunted. "All right," he finally said, looking down at Morris.

"Throw some water on his face, or what's left of it."

Wes took another deep breath, the cold air burning his lungs. The girl said something like "this will have to do," but Anderson wasn't paying much attention. He studied MacDermott and Livingston, both men looking over the unconscious Morris, ignoring Cora and him. The Nez Percé medicine man sat warming himself by the fire. Anderson's coat lay on the ground, his gun farther away, and the girl only had a wool blanket draped over her shoulders.

No food, no horses, no weapons. It wasn't much of a chance, Anderson thought, but this was as good as it might get. He looked up. "Can you run?"

Cora stared at him silently for a moment. She glanced quickly behind them, looked back at Wesley, and nodded. Anderson grabbed her hand and stood quickly. Without speaking, he pulled her forward and ran into the darkness.

A startled horse snorted, alerting MacDermott, and he heard the crashing of boots through the woods. He swore as he spun around, jerking a .45 from his sash. Paul Livingston rose and ran toward his Henry rifle as MacDermott's Colt boomed. Once. Twice. Three times. But by the time Livingston reached the Henry, Anderson and the girl had disappeared into the night.

Hohops laughed, but Livingston and MacDermott ignored him. With a curse, MacDermott shoved the revolver back into place and savagely kicked Morris's side. "Get up, you fool!" he shouted.

Anderson felt a sharp pain in his left side and knew he was falling. He managed to sling Cora past him as he dropped to his knees, sliding across the ground a few feet, breaking the fall with his right hand. "Go on," he said, but Cora stopped.

He knew he had been hit but wasn't sure how badly. His left side burned, and his shirt stuck to the skin. He pressed his hand against the wound, realized the bullet had only grazed him, and looked up as Cora ran back to him, ignoring the shouting from the camp, and pulled him to his feet by his shirt. "Get up!" she yelled, adding an oath that surprised Anderson despite the pain. Her thin right hand clamped onto his, and with a jerk, Wesley found himself stumbling on behind her as they ran into the night.

They blindly moved forward, tripping, gasping for breath until neither could go farther. Leaning against an earthen mound, Anderson managed to curb his loud breathing and listen. Nothing. For now, they were safe. But they couldn't wait long. He tried to swallow, but his throat was dry. Cora's teeth chattered, and he looked at her. Even in the darkness, he could see her shivering.

He put his arm over her shoulder and they both sank to the ground. "I'm . . . soooooooo . . . tired," she said softly. Anderson untied his bandanna and held it against his side, sticky and warm with blood.

His legs didn't want to cooperate, but Anderson made himself stand. He grimaced as he pulled Cora to her feet. "We can't stay here," he said. "Have to find a place to hide . . . for the night."

Neither had the strength to run, but Anderson didn't want to run. They'd move slow, now that they were away from the camp. Move quietly until they could find a cave or hollow or thicket—some place that would provide shelter.

He heard the running water long before they stepped into the stream. The creek felt icy, its coldness hurting their teeth as they drank with cupped hands. They were in a clearing now, because the moon and Milky Way lit up the sky and reflected off a mountain lake surrounded by forest and granite boulders. Even in the blackness of night, the place was beautiful.

Then he saw the beaver dam.

His mind flashed back. He saw himself rolling down the hill on the South Pass City road, crashing against the dam as MacDermott's men slaughtered Alec Dunbar's guards. Wes staggered back, partly from his loss of blood, partly from his memories. Cora grabbed his arm and whispered something. They both heard the voices.

"Over here! I think I heard something!"

It was Paul Livingston.

Anderson saw the light from a torch, picking its way through the forest, heading toward the lake.

Wesley cursed. *Anderson's luck!* The clearing offered no place to hide, and the light from the moon and stars lit up the place. They'd have to move. But where?

His eyes fell on the beaver dam.

He had barely been in Wyoming Territory when he first heard the story of mountain man John Colter. Before even Anderson's father had been born, Colter had made his way to the Wind River and Grand Tetons, discovered the geysers in the Yellowstone country, and had been wounded and captured by Blackfeet.

The Indians stripped Colter naked and told him to run for his life. They gave him a head start before pursuing. One Blackfoot threw his spear at Colter but missed, so the mountain man grabbed the weapon and charged the nearest Indian, killing him with his own weapon, then turning and running as fast as he could from the oncoming warriors.

He came to a pond and saw the beaver dam. Colter dived into the pond and took shelter in the beaver's lodge. He hid there until the Blackfeet gave up. About a week later, John Colter staggered into the nearest fort.

At least, that's what the legend said.

"Come on," Anderson whispered and stepped into the frigid water.

Cora gasped when she waded into the lake, but Anderson moved forward, clenching his jaw tight to keep his teeth from chattering. They reached the edge of the beaver's lodge. Cora couldn't keep herself from shivering.

Anderson caught his breath. "We'll go under, come up inside." He held her hands tightly and glanced at the bank. The light from the torches bobbed through the woods, closer now, heading toward them.

He nodded at Cora and both sank beneath the water.

They came up inside the wooden lodge, filling their lungs with air. Wesley reached with his left hand and gripped the side. He wrapped his right arm around Cora's shoulder and pulled her close. She couldn't stop shaking from the cold. He heard the angry chatter from a beaver on the other side of the lodge. He blinked water from his eyes and listened.

A few minutes passed. Maybe more. He couldn't tell. The beaver, or maybe there were two—Anderson was unsure in the blackness—quieted, apparently aware of a new threat. Wes heard the voices too.

"Well!"

It was MacDermott.

"I told you there's no way we're gonna find them in the dark, Vaughn!" Livingston said.

"I told you, Anderson's your responsibility!"

"Then you should have stopped Lane from trying to kill him!"

There were only two of them. That made sense. They would have left Morris back with Hohops and the horses, in case Wesley and Cora doubled back.

The voices died down. A rock splashed in the water nearby. One of them was taking out his frustrations.

"Let's go back to camp," MacDermott said quietly. "They'll die up here, and we still have that stupid Indian."

Footsteps faded away, and the beaver—no, there were two—resumed their angry banter, and one of them began swatting its tail against the side of the wooden lodge. Anderson sighed. Cora had fallen asleep against his chest. He'd stay longer in the beaver's place, just to play it safe. MacDermott might go on without them, as he said he would. Or maybe he'd try again at daybreak, make Hohops track them. Wesley had no illusions that they were free and safe. Hiding in the freezing waters had bought some time. But how much?

Chapter Thirteen

The bullet had glanced off one of Anderson's ribs and plowed an ugly furrow across his side, but soaking in cold water during the night in the beaver's lodge had slowed the bleeding. Now, at dawn, the blood had clotted. It looked ugly, but not fatal.

"You're lucky," Cora said, as she wrapped a make-shift bandage around Wesley's ribs.

Anderson snorted. "Never considered myself lucky," he said, and grimaced when Cora pulled tight on the piece of cotton she had torn from his shirt.

She squatted in front of him—Indian style; Wes liked that—and tried to comb her stringy, wet, and knotted hair with her fingers. Wes stood, stretched his muscles, and listened. Treetops rustled in the wind, and a fish jumped in the lake. Nothing sounded out of the ordinary. Anderson had debated with himself whether MacDermott would look for them or leave

116

them behind. He still wasn't certain one way or the other.

"Well," Cora said, and Wes turned to face her. "Shouldn't we get started?"

"Where?" Wesley asked. Maybe she had a plan.

"Down," she said firmly. "Back to South Pass City to fetch the law." Her face said she thought Wesley Anderson was the biggest idiot in the territory.

Anderson shook his head. "We can't make it down," he said.

Cora shot to her feet and shouted, "I knew it! I knew you'd want to go after that gold. You're a greedy—"

"Hey!" Anderson shot back. "How do you figure we'd make it back to South Pass City or even your cabin? Without any guns . . . no horses . . . no food. At best we starve to death. At worst, we get caught in a snowstorm and freeze to death."

She turned away from him, scooped up a rock, and sent it splashing into the water. "And what's your plan?" she said bitterly, her back to him. "How do you expect to get horses or guns from MacDermott? Sneak in? They'll be expecting that."

He shook his head. "All right," he said. "You want to go down by yourself, I won't stop you. Might be for the best anyway, in case you're right and I get killed."

Cora faced him now. Her eyes softened. "You told me you wouldn't risk my life for the gold," she said, hoping the tone didn't sound like she was pleading.

She wasn't. She was simply reminding him of his promise.

"I won't," he said. "But we need horses and guns. It's too far to walk."

"If they don't come after us, they'll expect us to go after them. MacDermott's no fool."

Anderson nodded. "He'll expect us to sneak up from behind," he said. The plan had just struck him. "But if we reach your father's camp first, we could surprise them."

He wondered if Breckenridge would have left a rifle or revolver at his camp. Probably not, but there might be some food—enough to give Cora and him some strength. And there would probably be some mining equipment. Breckenridge wouldn't want to haul all of his gear back to town and have to lug it up again. Maybe some blasting equipment. Dynamite. They could rig a trap. That was a long shot too, but there had to be some tools there. A pick or shovel.

Wes could envision it. MacDermott and Morris would be excited, off guard, when they rode in. Wesley would be waiting in the shadows. He'd ambush one with the pick; then Wesley would have a gun. If it worked, MacDermott and his men would be dead, Cora would be out of danger, and he'd be this close to Alec Dunbar's gold.

"Can you find your dad's camp?" he asked.

Cora laughed. "That's why I'm here, remember?"

Wes couldn't help but smile. "Would your dad have some supplies left up there, a rifle or pistol maybe?"

Cora shook her head. "No guns. He woulda took

those with him. Mostly all he would leave would be some mining gear, maybe some canned food and clothes. And his tent.'' She brightened, remembering. ''Pa was superstitious. If he found something, he wouldn't move his tent. Said that was bad luck.''

Smiling, Anderson said, ''My dad was the same way. Wear the same socks, britches, coat whenever he went hunting or fishing.''

He told her his plan, omitting his idea that they'd stay on and look for the fortune after MacDermott was dead, and she nodded in agreement. She didn't like the idea, Wes could tell, but she knew he was right, that they'd never make it back to civilization alive on foot.

''We'd better get moving,'' Anderson said.

''Can I ask you something?''

Anderson looked at her, then nodded. They were huddled inside a cave after hiking all day, staying off the main trail for fear of running into MacDermott or his men. Wes had tried for an hour to get a small fire going, but the makings were too wet, so now they had only their body heat to warm themselves in the cold night.

''Why is the gold so important to you?''

They had had this conversation before, so Wesley shrugged, not wanting to be drawn into the debate again. ''Why was it so important to your father?'' he asked instead. It sounded harsh. He immediately regretted his words, but Cora smiled.

''Pa thought he could buy my happiness. We never had nothing, 'specially after Ma died. Shucks, I was happy. I loved that cabin, those mountains. I did, at least. Don't reckon I'd want to go back there now that Pa's dead.''

That surprised Wesley. Not that she'd want to leave her home after her father's death, but that she hadn't left before. She was in her early twenties—practically a spinster by these frontier standards.

''Must have been lonely,'' he said, more out of curiosity than the need for conversation, ''growing up there.''

''Oh, it wasn't bad. During the boom years, we had neighbors, and once a month during spring and summer we'd go into town for supplies and such. I even attended school in South Pass for a couple of years.''

''No boyfriends?'' he asked. She looked at him. Maybe her eyes sparkled, or maybe it was just the moonlight playing tricks on him. Maybe it was only wishful thinking.

''Shoshone braves dropped by a couple of times and offered Pa a dozen horses to marry me. Pa said I was worth two dozen, so I stayed single. And you, Wesley Anderson. How come you ain't hitched?''

''Four years in prison,'' he said. ''Remember?''

''And before that?''

He shook his head. ''Been drifting since I was a teenager,'' he answered.

''You didn't leave some girl sobbing back in . . .''

''Jefferson, Texas,'' he said. ''Nope. All the girls in Jefferson were probably glad to see me leave anyway.''

''What was it like? Jefferson, I mean.''

He tried to think back that far. How long had it been

since he had thought about Jefferson? The past four years he had thought of nothing but his bad luck, Dunbar's gold, and trying to survive prison. Before that, he tried not to recall the past.

Jefferson lay on Big Cypress Bayou. His father owned a lumber mill, and his older brother worked in the nearby iron ore smelters. Wesley worked briefly in Noble Birge's hardware store. Brother Andy had given him grief over that: sweeping up the store and selling penny candy to the girls while Andy and Papa sweated and groaned and labored like mules in real jobs for real men. Then came the War, and Wesley Anderson had to grow up in a hurry.

But Jefferson? What was the town like? It was a city—got even bigger after he left—a river town, and he could remember the steamboats coming in all the way from New Orleans, sometimes as many as fifteen docked, and bales of cotton stacked two stories high. . . .

"And mosquitoes the size of ravens," Anderson concluded.

Cora laughed. "They get to be crow-size here in the summer," she said.

"How well I know."

They were silent for a minute. The wind picked up, and a cloud soon blocked the moon, darkening the cave.

"You never answered my question," she said.

He rubbed his eyes. "I told you before. Wyoming owes me something for the four years I spent in prison."

"No," she said. "That's not it. You might tell yourself that's the reason, but it's not."

"Then what is it?" he asked testily.

"I don't know. But I think you do."

Go to sleep, he thought, but didn't say it out loud. Why did he want that fortune? It was a lot of money, sure, but was it worth dying for, was it worth getting caught and being sent back to Laramie? He could be halfway to Texas by now, free, or in Montana.

Anderson's luck.

And there he had the answer.

For years, Wesley Anderson had nothing. Papa said he was too small and too young to work in the lumber mill, smelters, plow works, or even on the docks. Then Papa, caught up in the fervent patriotism of the new Confederacy, sold his lumber mill to raise a regiment for Texas. And Wesley was too young and too small to fight, so he had been left behind, as his brother and father marched off to fight, and die, for a cause itself that would soon be dead and defeated.

His mother made him flee Texas to escape the War, so he left them behind. Mother died of fever in '71—his sister had written him, though it took seven months for the letter to catch up—and Sissy had married some Yankee who was working for Jefferson's ammonia refrigerant ice plant, whatever that was.

So Wes worked hard just to eat, and there were times when he didn't eat. He had sweated and cursed as a teamster, ridden shotgun for a stagecoach company, been a cowboy, traded with the Nez Percé, slaved away in the mines, livery stables, even served as a deputy sheriff and found himself sweeping out a mercantile again and selling penny candy.

And finally he had his chance. The pouch of gold Alec Dunbar offered him held more money than Wes had ever seen. It could buy a new beginning. Only Anderson's luck struck again, and took everything— Wesley's hopes and dreams and last chance—away. Now he was back after Dunbar's fortune.

It had nothing to do with justice. Wyoming had made a terrible mistake by sending him to the penitentiary, but the territory didn't owe Wesley Anderson one hundred thousand dollars. Cora Breckenridge had been right.

Wesley Anderson was greedy. As bad as MacDermott's marauders, and probably worse. Vaughn MacDermott offered no excuses as to why he wanted the gold.

They left the cave at dawn, moving without speaking. A few hours later, they topped a rise and stopped. The way down was marred by loose shale and gravel, but in the distance, Anderson could make out a narrow pass. He pointed it out to Cora. It was a slim trail, pass probably wouldn't describe it, but Anderson could vaguely make out the semblance of a gunsight. After all, to him the Rabbit Ears in New Mexico Territory near Texas never resembled their namesake. But Cora recognized it in an instant, and she nodded and smiled, reflecting on better times with her father. Sadness suddenly enveloped her and she looked down.

Anderson studied the surroundings. It looked clear, so he eased his way down the steep grade, slowly at first, then picking up speed as he descended, sliding, kicking up dust and gravel with Cora right behind him. He hit the base and fell forward, groaning as pain raced through his side. Cora helped him up, and he felt his wound, relieved that it hadn't started bleeding again. He rubbed his skinned hands on his pants, and they walked toward Gunsight Pass.

It was a high-walled, narrow trail, with room for only one horse. Old dung and an empty tin of beans told him he was right. Horace Breckenridge had been here. After examining the ground carefully, Anderson saw something he didn't like, something he should have noticed before. Fresh tracks were hard to read on rocky ground, but horse manure wasn't.

He looked up quickly. "What is it?" Cora asked, and Anderson told her. Poring over the trail, he tried to remember everything he had been taught about tracking. He swore softly and stood up. MacDermott and his men had been through earlier. But maybe they hadn't found Breckenridge's camp.

Cautiously Cora and Anderson moved forward. The rocky walls would be perfect for an ambush, Anderson thought as they rounded a bend, but there was no other way—at least, none that he could tell. The path looked clear, so they moved on, then stopped at the metallic, cold sound of a rifle being cocked.

Wesley Anderson turned and saw Paul Livingston, hidden deep in the rocks, grinning as if he held the winning hand at a poker table. With the Henry rifle, in many ways he did.

"Howdy, partner," Livingston said. "Been waiting for you."

Chapter Fourteen

Cora and Anderson slowly walked toward the far side of the pass, where MacDermott had made temporary camp. Livingston followed, the Henry rifle resting easily on his shoulders.

"Figured you would come looking for the old man's camp," Livingston told his captives nonchalantly, then abruptly changed the subject: "You know, partner, I've saved your life at least a half-dozen times."

"How so?" Anderson said, obviously not interested in Livingston's banter.

"Well, I could have killed you in the livery back in South Pass. But then I decided to arrest you and frame you for the murder. A hanging, at least, would bring a bit of excitement to town. Place has been dead and boring for some time now. That was the original plan, for me to take word to Cora and let her know her father was being planted up on the hill, knowing of course that Cora would be with Vaughn and the others. I'd just catch up with them.

"But then, I heard your story, and I figured this was better. I left word in town that you and I were going to break the news to Cora, then go after the men that killed her pa."

Anderson nodded, understanding. He could appreciate the plan. No one in South Pass City would come after them, unless some old church lady decided to help Breckenridge's grieving daughter—and considering the miner's reputation in town, and the dearth of old church ladies in western Wyoming Territory, that was far from likely.

"So you didn't resign," Anderson said flatly. He didn't mean it as a question; he already knew the answer.

Livingston laughed. "Nah," he said. "If I resign, I wouldn't be much help to Vaughn. Nope, this way, no one thinks to go looking for Cora." He paused for a minute, collecting his thoughts, before continuing. "Let's see. Where was I? Oh, yeah, I'm counting the times I saved your hide. That's twice. Then when you 'rescued' Cora. I could have killed you then, and later I stopped Lane from cutting you in half. That's five times."

"Four," Anderson corrected.

"Four times. Right. But Vaughn was ready to kill you after you beat up Lane. So that's five times. And I could have shot you a couple of minutes ago. Yup, that's a half-dozen times." He shook his head and corrected himself.

"Seven. I could have let you drown in the river when y'all tried to escape."

Wesley had never heard Livingston talk so much. He was chattering on incessantly like a teenage boy, excited. The Mississippian seemed to realize this himself because he suddenly cleared his throat and lowered his voice.

"Anyway, partner," he continued, finally getting to his point, "for reasons I don't care to discuss, I'd like to keep you alive. But if you keep pulling stunts like fighting Lane and running off with little Cora, I'll be hard-pressed to keep you in one piece."

They were at the edge of the camp, and Livingston brought the rifle forward. MacDermott and Morris were sitting on a boulder, and Cora and Anderson smiled at each other when they saw Morris's black-and-blue face. Hohops knelt near the animals, his eyes shut and a woolen blanket draped over his bony shoulders.

MacDermott stood and angrily approached the captives. Livingston shot out in a pleading voice, "Vaughn, Wesley here has agreed to help us scout some more and promises not to run off."

It sounded lame, Wes thought. *It was lame.*

"That's too bad," MacDermott said, and he drew his gun.

Anderson braced himself for the bullet, but Livingston stepped in front of him, clenching the Henry tightly and raising his voice: "Vaughn, we need him! Lane lost the old man's trail and chances are once we find the camp, we'll still need Anderson. Look." He pointed to the ominous, dark clouds. "It'll snow soon, and we have to be off this mountain before it does, else we'll die up here with Lee Thorn and all the others. We've waited too long for this . . . we're too close now to Dunbar's gold.''

Slowly Vaughn MacDermott eased the Colt back into the sash, and Anderson swallowed. Morris slowly stood, putting his right palm on the butt of his revolver.

''We don't need the girl,'' he said dryly. ''We found the pass without her help.''

''If you kill her, you'd better kill me too!'' Anderson shouted, surprised he could talk at all and even more shocked at what he had said.

Morris grinned. ''That's fine with me.''

Tension hung over the camp like thick smoke.

''Kill them all,'' Hohops said suddenly in a soft but forceful voice. The ancient *tewat*'s eyes bore directly into MacDermott. ''We must all soon join the men you murdered, *kap-seese*. Why prolong our pitiful lives here on the Mother Earth when we can become part of the soil?''

MacDermott screamed, ''Shut up! All of you, shut up!'' He turned and glared at Morris, who hesitantly took his hand off the gun and sat back down. For a minute, the only sound was the wind. Finally, MacDermott looked at Livingston.

''All right, Paul, we keep them alive for now. But if they try anything else, I let Lane have the both of 'em.'' He stepped to the side and looked Anderson in the eye. ''And the girl goes first and we make you watch.'' MacDermott turned quickly, kicked a small stone at his feet, and walked away.

Hohops chuckled. A horse snorted.

Paul Livingston faced Anderson and smiled.

"Eight times," he said. "If you're a cat, you'd better tread softly."

Finding Breckenridge's trail proved difficult, for wind and rain had eliminated most sign. To give up was to invite death, so Anderson continued studying the ground. Even so, he still almost missed spotting the brush collected at the base of the trail on the side of the canyon.

It was an animal trail, and someone had gone to great effort to hide it. The path led up, disappearing into the rocks and trees. Like Gunsight Pass itself, it seemed barely big enough for a man and a mule, and Anderson motioned MacDermott and the others forward. Twenty to thirty yards up, he discovered an old clay pipe stem, slightly buried in the ground, and an overturned stone. Those were enough to go on.

"You're a pretty good tracker, partner," Livingston said. "Where did you pick it up?"

"Half-breed Cheyenne teamster I worked with," he said. "Also spent some time with the Nez Percé." He looked up, studied an aspen and moved curiously to it, feeling the scarred bark well above his head.

"What's that?"

"Grizzly sign," he said. "Big one, I'd guess."

"Really?" Livingston studied the mark, impressed like a grade-school kid.

"The grizzly is my spirit," Hohops said and admired the bear's claw marks.

MacDermott, however, had no interest in nature or

Nez Percé superstition. "Move it," he ordered, and swore underneath his breath.

They continued up, cleared the top, and slowly picked their way ahead. Around dusk, at the base of a clearing, Anderson noticed something white. A short while later, he clearly saw the canvas tent flapping in the breeze, obviously unused for weeks.

It was Breckenridge's base camp, all right, and he had left it in a hurry, anxious to get off the mountain for more supplies or something. They pitched camp, picketed their animals, and looked around. In a canvas war bag, Anderson dug out some frayed long johns and shaving tools. MacDermott jerked the satchel from his hands and looked inside, then, exasperated, he handed it back to Anderson.

No map, no claim. Breckenridge wouldn't need to file a claim; the gold he sought had been mined years ago. Anderson glanced at the dirt floor and saw the crude drawing in the ground that Breckenridge must have sketched weeks before. It looked to be . . .

"A cave," Paul Livingston said, peering over Anderson's shoulder.

"I told you of the cave," Hohops said.

But where was it?

It was too late in the day to look for a cave, but Morris and MacDermott went out anyway, leaving Livingston to watch over the camp. Hohops brought his ceremonial wing to his face and began chanting some Nez Percé song. Cora fixed supper, Anderson gathered firewood, and both studied their options; neither liked them.

Now that they had found the base camp, Mac-Dermott had little reason to keep them alive, except as common laborers. Paul Livingston wouldn't be able to keep them alive forever. Wes wondered if Livingston would be able to stay alive himself. He doubted it. MacDermott would murder everyone, including Morris and Livingston, to keep the fortune for himself. That had to be why Paul worked so hard to keep Anderson alive. It certainly had nothing to do with friendship or being "partners."

The wind whipped savagely through the camp, a bitter, biting blast of arctic air that chilled everyone. Thunder rumbled in the distance, and Anderson shivered, not from the cold, but rather the prospect of a wet, freezing night with only a mildewed canvas tent for cover.

Rain began sprinkling shortly thereafter, then started falling harder until it became a cold torrent blown every which way by the winter wind. If the temperature dropped another ten degrees, the rain would become sleet. If an early blizzard struck, they'd find themselves stuck on this mountain with nothing to do but die.

The cook fire was put out before supper could be finished, so Livingston, Anderson, Cora, and Hohops moved inside the tent to wait out the storm. Cora made Wesley remove his shirt and redressed the bullet wound, and Livingston sighed and reluctantly handed her a pewter flask. She took the flask, and Livingston shrugged.

"Whiskey," he said, "probably enough left to give that a decent cleaning."

Livingston turned quickly, staring intently outside. He cocked his rifle and swallowed hard. "You hear that?"

The only sound for a moment was the pounding of the rain, which suddenly became hail, and then, above the noise of the storm, all four heard it:

Laughter.

Seconds turned to minutes, and minutes seemed like hours as they waited, shaking inside the tent as the storm beat on without mercy. Something flashed in the distance, and Livingston raised the Henry.

Anderson found himself holding his breath, wishing he had his revolver. Something gripped his arm, and he realized it was Cora, her fingers white against his forearm. She bit her lip in fear. The wind howled. Hohops mumbled a prayer, maybe his death song, and suddenly Paul Livingston cursed savagely.

Vaughn MacDermott and Lane Morris splashed through the mud and into the tent, laughing hard and panting.

"You scared us half to death!" Livingston said, sinking to a seated position.

"Didn't know you were such a woman," Mac-Dermott said after he caught his breath. He smiled, reached into his coat pocket, and withdrew a chunk of rusty metal and set it before them. It was an old frame to a large revolver, what appeared to have been a Colt's Dragoon.

"It's Lee Thorn's," MacDermott said. "Has to be. And we found it half-buried with a couple of bones from a horse."

"Could belong to any miner or trapper," Livingston offered, but MacDermott shook his head violently.

"It has to be Thorn's. With the horse bones." He shivered and offered his theory: Thorn, badly wounded, had driven the hearse as far as it could go into the mountains. Next, he unhitched the team, loaded the gold on one or more horses, and led the animals into the mountains. Then he buried the gold in a cave and died.

It made sense. A prospector had found the hearse wrecked at the base of the mountains in the fall of '74 but no horses, no gold, and no Lee Thorn. Anderson studied the ancient, corroded revolver. If it were the frame of Thorn's Dragoon, if Breckenridge had been right about the cave and the gold, then Wesley and Cora were close.

Close to Dunbar's fortune . . . and being murdered by Vaughn MacDermott.

Chapter Fifteen

MacDermott was up before dawn the next morning, off on a short scout before Livingston had Cora cooking breakfast. Morris slid his knife across his whetstone, Hohops checked on the stock, and Anderson sat playing the pennywhistle, first "The Prisoner's Hope" then "The Yellow Rose of Texas." He had just started an Irish ballad he had picked up in the Laramie prison when MacDermott returned. The hard frown and creased forehead told everyone that the outlaw's search had turned up nothing.

They were low on grub. The bacon strips were sliced thin, and the coffee tasted like dyed water. MacDermott told Livingston to try to find some game, maybe a mountain goat or elk, while Morris would stay behind and guard the prisoners. MacDermott himself would make another scout for the hidden cave Breckenridge had found.

"I don't care much for that plan," Morris said, emptying the dregs from his tin cup.

MacDermott returned the killer's icy glare. "I don't rightly care what you think, Lane. That's the way it's going to be."

Morris shook his head. "What's to stop you from hidin' that gold once you find it, Major?" he asked. MacDermott only smiled. "Or what's to stop him"— he nodded at Livingston—"from huntin' for gold rather than grub and doin' the same." MacDermott's eyes hardened as he considered those odds.

"Paul could pick us all off with that Henry rifle of his, once he found Dunbar's fortune," Morris added.

"You're a fool, Lane," Livingston said.

The morning turned quiet.

"All right," MacDermott finally said. "Paul and you'll go hunting for food this morning. I'll stay in camp and make our friends here chop some firewood, get this place in shape. This afternoon, Paul and I'll go out and you'll stay guard. Paul will pull guard duty tomorrow morning and you and I'll make the rounds. We'll rotate the shifts. One man in camp. Two scouting. Always. Nobody leaves camp alone. Agreed?"

Morris and Livingston nodded and departed shortly afterward. Wesley and Hohops made a stronger rope corral for the animals, while Cora straightened her father's tent and made a makeshift lean-to. By noon, when Lane and Paul had still not returned, Vaughn MacDermott paced around the camp anxiously, rubbing the palms of his hands against his trousers, mumbling something under his breath.

Wesley squatted by the fire and poured himself a cup of weak coffee. Cora sat beside him and glanced at Hohops, who lay curled up underneath the lean-to. MacDermott had spent more time looking for his partners to return than he had watching his prisoners.

"They don't trust each other," Cora said softly.

Anderson smiled. "Gold fever," he said. "With any luck, they'll kill each other over it and we'll have it all to ourselves."

Cora turned toward him and snapped, "I don't care about that gold. It means nothing to me but death."

Frowning, Anderson apologized. He stared at the fire for a minute before looking back at Cora.

"I'm sorry," she said.

Wes shook his head. "Not your fault. I shouldn't have said it." He realized she was reaching for him, and he pulled her close. She shivered and bowed her head against his shoulder. Wesley reached up with his right hand awkwardly and stroked her hair. Cora wasn't crying—she was too strong for that; at least, she wouldn't cry again in front of MacDermott.

But this . . . Wesley whispered, "It'll all work out, Cora." He knew how she felt. Forced to stay in her father's camp, surrounded by the memories, with the very men who had murdered him and would, in all probability, kill her too. He felt her shudder once, and then she straightened, wiped her eyes, and stared at him.

Wesley took her hands in his own. Cora slowly leaned forward and kissed him softly. She pulled away and smiled. "You're a sweetheart, Wesley. Thank you."

She was gone, back inside the tent. Anderson stared at MacDermott. The killer stood in the far end of camp, leaning against a tree, staring into the distance looking for his partners. Wesley measured the distance mentally. He could race across the camp and tackle the major, disarm him, and ambush Livingston and Morris when they returned. He'd have to kill Lane; of this, Wesley was certain. But then he'd have Paul and MacDermott prisoners and he could get Cora off the mountain and back to safety.

Wesley smiled suddenly. He hadn't even considered Alec Dunbar's gold. Maybe there was hope for him yet. Slowly he stood, glanced quickly at the sleeping Nez Percé holy man, and stepped around the fire pit. He swallowed, crouched . . . and heard the hurried footsteps of Livingston and Morris returning to camp.

"What took you so long?" MacDermott snapped.

They nooned on hardtack and coffee, for the hunters had returned empty-handed. Paul and MacDermott prepared to leave, and Anderson offered his services as a tracker. This MacDermott quickly rejected. "You stay in camp," he said. "Where we can watch you better."

"We wouldn't have to watch them if they were dead," Morris said.

MacDermott studied it, but finally shook his head. "For now, we let them live," he said. "Chop some firewood. We'll be back before dusk."

But they weren't back. Black clouds darkened the sky as Wesley chopped some rotting wood and stacked it at the edge of camp. The horses and mules stamped their feet and moved around the corral nervously, and Wesley smelled sulfur in the air. A bluish ball danced on the edge of the ax blade, and he quickly pitched the tool to the ground.

Startled, he let out a curse and backed away. The hole stack of wood glowed eerily now. He saw the balls of light on the mules's ears, also. Even his hatband glowed. The air remained still as he backed away from the bright wood, aware of the sweat dampening his face and shirt.

"What's goin' on?" Morris yelled from the tent.

Hohops began his death song.

The sky turned darker. A ball of light rolled across the camp, and the horses whinnied and bolted to the far side of the corral. The ropes wouldn't be able to hold the animals if they spooked. Wesley hoped the glowing wood would keep the livestock pinned back in the makeshift corral, prayed that the horses would be too scared to run past the terrifying silvery blue light.

"What is it?" Morris screamed again.

Foxfire. Wesley knew this, but his throat was too dry to speak. He was at the tent now, and ducked inside. Hohops sang from the lean-to. Anderson felt Cora grab his hand as they stared outside.

He had heard about the silvery glow emitted from rotting wood, but had never seen it firsthand. Likewise, cattlemen and old sailors had told him about Saint Elmo's fire, the luminous blue light during electrical storms that appeared on mastheads, cattle horns, the ears of livestock, even clothes and tools. His fingers interlocked with Cora's, and they both jumped when a bolt of lightning split the sky.

The rain came quickly, icy but relieving, and the blue light died. The woodpile, however, continued to glow. Hohops still sang.

"Where's Vaughn?" Morris asked. He talked to hear himself speak. Fear etched itself across the cold-blooded assassin's face. The Nez Percé's song did nothing to lessen this. Wesley wondered if he could disarm Morris now, but the killer seemed to sense this and turned quickly, drawing the Navy Colt and thumbing back the hammer.

"Back up!" Morris shouted.

Anderson did as he was told but said softly, "I'd put the gun away, Lane. I've heard of cowboys on drives getting fried by lightning during storms like this."

The rain stopped as quickly as it had begun. The evening air fell still again, though much colder, and the woodpile glowed. Morris motioned with the revolver barrel, and Wesley led Cora outside. They stopped suddenly, staring at the brush rustling at the edge of camp.

Hohops ended his song and moved in front of them, mumbling something in his native tongue that Wes couldn't understand. The ancient *tewat* approached the quaking brush and stopped. The rain had put out the fire, so the only light came from the silvery foxfire.

"Hohops," Cora called out. "Be careful."

Wesley turned to Morris. "You've got a gun. Go help him. That might be a wolf—or a bear!"

Suddenly, Hohops let out a scream. He turned and sprinted toward the horses.

"Stop!" Morris shouted, but on the holy man ran.

Lane raised his gun. "No!" Wesley stepped forward, but a crash of thunder and lightning drowned out his cry as well as the report of the Colt. Hohops staggered and fell heavily across the ropes.

Anderson turned savagely at Morris, shoving Cora aside for her own protection. "You son of a—"

He never finished his curse or charge. Something big bolted out of the brush. Wesley heard the footsteps, Cora's scream, and he saw the fear in Lane Morris's widening eyes. Wesley remembered the grizzly sign he had pointed out to Livingston. Morris turned and ran, dropping the Navy Colt into the mud. Anderson's eyes fell on the revolver, but one didn't fight a bear with a .36-caliber pistol, and he didn't have enough time to grab the Colt anyway.

"Wesley!" Cora shouted.

The breath left his lungs as something crashed into Anderson's back. He landed heavily and slid through the mud. Vaguely he noticed the horses and mules galloping past, saw the flash of lightning in the sky, the shimmer of silver light from the woodpile.

Something fell on top of him.

Wes clamped his eyes shut and groaned with pain. He heard Cora yell for help, waited for the claws to rip him apart or some beast's fangs to tear into his throat—but this didn't happen. It was impossible to breathe as giant hands crushed his throat. Anderson opened his eyes and struggled fruitlessly at what was atop him.

A quick succession of lightning flashes lit up the sky, and Anderson saw his attacker clearly. He was a giant in bearskins, with unruly hair to his waist and a white beard that flowed across his chest. His face was scarred and burned dark from the sun and wind, and only a few teeth remained. The man-beast growled like a bear and Anderson struggled to free his right hand, then jabbed a fist into the man's side with little effect.

Suddenly Cora was beside him, slapping and clawing at the man's face, but he released his grip on Anderson's throat with his left hand and tossed her effortlessly away. Anderson turned then to see Morris frozen in shock at the tent. A giant fist pounded Anderson's head and his vision blurred.

"Help him!" Cora screamed at Morris, but the gunman couldn't move.

Anderson looked up again at the hideous man atop him. Lightning flashed again. Wesley's vision cleared and he focused on the man's enraged face, saliva drooling from his mouth and one eye staring intently at him; the other eye wandered about as if checking for other attackers. Then Cora swung the tree limb with all her might and broke it over the wild man's head. He wasn't invincible after all, Anderson thought, as the man groaned and released his grip on Anderson's throat. Cora swung again with her now-shorter stick and knocked the man to his side.

After sucking cold air into his lungs, Anderson crawled rapidly toward the loaded Colt. He heard the man-beast roar once, then heavy footsteps pounded after him. With a final lunge, Anderson grabbed the butt of his revolver, rolled over, and cocked the hammer.

Lightning struck nearby. "Nooooooooooooooooooo!" the wild man screamed, his good eye wild in fright as he slid to a stop.

The revolver boomed, but Anderson knew he had missed as he jerked the trigger. Before he could cock the gun again, the man had taken off into the woods, streaking past the glowing wood, crashing through the bushes with the speed of a grizzly.

Slowly Anderson lowered his gun and tried to catch his breath. Cora ran over and knelt beside him, their hearts racing with fear even though the attacker was long gone. Footsteps and shouts sounded behind them.

"Put the gun down!" It was Paul Livingston's voice. Anderson was too exhausted to argue. He placed the Colt on the ground and rolled over, each breath short and painful.

MacDermott arrived shortly after, and the two men eased into the camp toward Morris, still frozen in his stance, eyes glazed over and face ashen. "What's going on here?" MacDermott shouted. "Where are the horses?"

Livingston lowered his rifle, leaned it against a tree, and cautiously approached Morris. The killer was almost in shock. He put his hand on Morris's shoulder and asked, "Lane, what is it? What happened?"

Lane Morris blinked once, and his lower lip trembled. His Adam's apple bobbed once, and the killer finally spoke in a subdued voice:

"It was Lee Thorn."

Chapter Sixteen

June 1873

The black hearse bounded over the hill, tilted to the left, and righted itself as the bear of a driver lashed out with a whip at the horses. The horses had been running for miles now and were foaming with sweat, a few were bleeding from their nostrils, all on the verge of collapsing.

Lee Thorn reined to a stop, exploding in a guttural laugh as he waited for the dozen riders to catch up. He reached into his coat pocket and pulled out a plug of tobacco, tore off a piece with his teeth, and glanced at the thunderheads over the mountains to his left. A good summer thunderstorm would wash away their tracks.

Then he began to hum.

He wore buckskins, a big dust-colored slouch hat, and a pair of Colt Dragoon .44s—giant horse pistols meant to be carried in saddle holsters, not strapped across a man's waist. His hair was red, long and flowing, with a graying beard that had not been trimmed or washed in years. His mere presence would unnerve most men, but to top it off, he had a wandering left eye that made his appearance even more menacing.

Riders began arriving, letting their horses catch their wind, but they stayed mounted, holding revolvers and rifles at the ready. Jonathan Vaughn MacDermott was the last to arrive. MacDermott eased over toward the hearse, looked up at his partner, and smiled.

Lee Thorn stopped humming, returned the grin, and asked, "Lose anyone?"

"A few. More money for us, right?"

Thorn grunted. He wouldn't have cared if all of MacDermott's Marauders had been killed—with the exception of MacDermott and him, of course—as long as they got the gold.

MacDermott patted the side of the hearse and considered his partner.

They were as opposite as cattle and sheep. As far as Vaughn MacDermott knew, Lee Thorn had been born in the Rocky Mountains, the offspring of some free trapper and either a Crow—or a Blackfoot, once in a while a Cheyenne—woman or one of the painted ladies the Saint Louis buyers brought to some rendezvous site in the '20s. The story depended on how many jugs of forty-rod whiskey Thorn had consumed. Sometimes he said he was raised by a she-wolf.

Vaughn MacDermott was a native of Connecticut, but had moved south just before the outbreak of the

War. He had served in the Confederacy for a few years before heading for the gold fields of western Montana.

Some said he was a major in the Confederate cavalry—indeed, most of his riders called him either Major or Mr. MacDermott out of respect, but mostly fear—but deserted after Gettysburg when he realized the cause was lost. In truth, however, he was an infantry private who had deserted long before Gettysburg to escape certain court-martial and execution when he shot and killed a young drummer boy who had accidentally spilled MacDermott's cup of coffee.

In little more than a year, Jonathan Vaughn MacDermott, Connecticut native, Confederate deserter, gentleman and murderer, had formed a notorious band of outlaws that owned the roads from the mining camps to Salt Lake City. Then he had fled the vigilantes to try his hand in Wyoming.

All he really knew about Lee Thorn was that the man was a killer, as vicious as Lane Morris, but completely mad. Thorn's ruthlessness had kept him alive for years. To be honest, Lee Thorn scared Vaughn MacDermott, but now the old mountain man's mind had been poisoned by insanity. And Vaughn MacDermott wasn't about to stretch a hangman's rope because of his crazy partner.

"Harry, you, Paul, Christian, and Tillis come with me. We'll ride back a ways, make sure we aren't being followed, then catch up with the others at Dead Man's Gully. The rest of you go with Lee."

At the command, Lee Thorn's whip cracked and the horses, despite being winded, bolted away in fear of their driver. The remaining riders followed, except one who hung back for a minute. MacDermott looked at him for a moment before nodding slightly.

Lane Morris grinned, understanding, and spurred his horse after the others.

Thunder, heavy and ominous, rolled in the distance and MacDermott turned to Lonesome Harry and asked, "Got a bottle to celebrate?"

"Ain't we gonna check the roads, make sure we ain't being followed?"

"Dead men can't follow us, and it'll be hours before their bodies are found and a posse is organized." MacDermott turned to Livingston. "But Paul, you and Tillis ride back a couple miles just to make sure."

"Then why don't we go with Thorn?" Harry said. "I don't like the idea of us being separated from that gold."

"Because," MacDermott said firmly as he swung from his horse. *Because I don't want to see an old friend die.*

The wind was picking up, the skies darkening as the hearse rolled into Dead Man's Gully. Thorn set the brake, but stayed atop the rig, as Lane Morris dismounted and walked to the rear door of the wagon. He drew his revolver, a heavy Remington Army .44, checked the percussion caps, and opened the door.

"Well, lookie here," Morris said, smiling as he disappeared into the hearse. Seconds later, a body flew out of the wagon and crashed to the ground. Morris reappeared shortly afterward.

"The gold's in the back, and I guess this is a bit of

a bonus," Morris said. The man was facedown on the dirt, so Morris kicked him over.

He was an old man, bleeding profusely from bullet wounds in his shoulder, leg, and side, dying most likely, but for the moment very much alive. He directed vile words in a heavy Scottish accent at the outlaws, prompting laughter from all of them, especially Lee Thorn, who always enjoyed a good joke.

"Mr. Dunbar," Morris said, "we thank you for deliverin' us some spendin' money."

Alec Dunbar's cold eyes locked on Morris as he sat upright, biting his lip in pain. His voice, cold and deliberate, silenced the outlaws's laughs: "I swear as I die that ye'll never have this gold. I curse ye and shall see to it."

"Dunbar," Morris answered, "we already got it." The Remington boomed, and Dunbar slammed to the ground with a bullet in his forehead.

Thorn grunted his approval and began to hum again. Morris nodded at the men on horseback, who dismounted, letting their mounts graze, and he walked around to face Thorn. He cocked the revolver again and pointed it at the giant driving the hearse. "Lee," he said, "why don't you slowly get down off that hearse." It was an order, not a request.

Lee Thorn's good eye stared at Morris, then at the others. His humming stopped, and he spit a stream of brown tobacco juice at Morris's feet. "You can't cross Major MacDermott," Thorn said. "He'll track you down and feed you to the buzzards."

"I ain't crossin' the major," Morris said. "He's endin' your partnership."

Realization slowly came to Thorn, and he stood as if to leap from the driver's seat, shifted directions, and came up with a Dragoon in his right hand—surprisingly quick for a man of his size. The revolver boomed simultaneously with a thunderclap and a heavy ball slammed into the solid brass buckle on Morris's gun belt, knocking the gunman to the ground with a loud grunt.

Thorn's handheld cannon exploded again and dropped another raider. The men's mounts, not picketed, galloped away at the gunshots; even the winded horses pulling the hearse managed to drag the heavy wagon a few yards despite the set brake.

One gunman drew his pistol and shot Thorn twice in the stomach, but the giant seemed unfazed by the wounds and killed his assailant with a head shot. That sent the remaining outlaws into a panic, and they chased after their horses only to be dropped by Thorn's deadly aim.

Faceup, groaning, but alive, Lane Morris realized he still gripped his Remington. He brought the gun up, steadying it with both hands, and fired at Thorn twice. Both bullets hit their mark and drove Thorn into a sitting position on the hearse, but he was far from finished. He released the brake, fired a shot at the horses's feet, scaring the already tormented animals into a gallop, pulling the hearse out of Dead Man's Gully and toward the mountains.

Lane Morris struggled to his feet, slowly cocked his revolver, and fired another shot. He saw dust pop from Thorn's back as the bullet hit, dropping Thorn out of sight as the hearse rolled on.

Holstering his pistol, Morris looked around, staring silently at the bodies of his dead comrades. He checked the now-dented buckle that had saved his life when the heavy ball ricocheted off the brass oval. It would leave a bruise, but no blood.

At least, not until MacDermott found out that Thorn had gotten away in the hearse. With the gold.

Rain pelted men and horses as they staggered toward the high mountains. Clouds blotted out the sun, and nightfall rapidly approached. MacDermott and his surviving men had lost the hearse's trail miles back, but the major was pushing them on, obsessed with the one hundred thousand dollars he had held in his grasp.

They took shelter for a minute beneath a line of trees and regrouped. MacDermott dismounted and peered up at the mountains, knowing that's where Thorn had to be. Before turning to outlawry, Lee Thorn had lived in those mountains, trapping, hunting, trading with Indians long before gold was discovered and white men had flocked to build towns and mines and make or lose fortunes.

Thorn ought to have died already, the horses should have given out long before they reached the mountains, and Thorn wouldn't be able to get the hearse through the trees and up the steep grade.

But Lee Thorn was the toughest man MacDermott ever met, almost impossible to kill. He knew every creek, crevice, and cave in those mountains, and he would somehow manage to take the gold up high and hide it, then crawl away like a wounded dog, laughing as he died at foiling MacDermott's plan.

Tillis swore to himself and dismounted.

"Get on your horse!" MacDermott ordered, but the gunman shook his head. They stared at each other, but the tension was broken when Paul Livingston galloped over the ridge and slid his horse to a stop.

"Posse!" Paul shouted.

MacDermott swore.

"Major," Morris said, "we gotta give this up for now."

Tillis's head nodded in agreement, and Lonesome Harry added, "We can't look for Thorn and hide from the law at the same time. Thorn's dead. He has to be. We'll—"

"If we leave now, someone else will grab that gold," MacDermott said.

Paul Livingston glanced behind him and spoke in a calm, reasoning voice: "The gold won't do us any good if we're dead."

MacDermott knew his men were right. Tillis had already climbed back in the saddle. Defeated, Vaughn MacDermott nodded and tugged on the reins. They rode north, toward Montana, away from the posse, away from one hundred thousand dollars in gold.

Chapter Seventeen

September 1877

It was hard to accept, impossible to believe. But with the wandering eye and the size of the man—it had to be Lee Thorn. He had somehow survived his wounds, managed to live high in these mountains for four years. *Four years.*

But how? And why?

The three outlaws surrounded a roaring campfire that night, while Cora sat in the tent with Hohops. The slug from the .36 had smashed into the Indian's back, punctured a lung, and cracked a rib on its way through the chest. Cora bathed the old man's sweaty forehead, wiped bloody froth from his lips, and listened to the sucking sound he made with each struggling breath. She could do nothing else; she knew Hohops lay dying.

Wes squeezed her shoulder gently. "You all right?"

Cora nodded.

"Call me if you need me," he said, and stepped into the cold night to join the outlaws by the fire. He looked at the woodpile, still silvery, and listened as MacDermott related his double cross of Lee Thorn.

"It can't be," he said when he had finished.

"It was him," Morris said. "I'd know that face anywhere."

"You really think he'd live up in these mountains like some hermit with a fortune in gold?" Livingston said in disbelief.

"He's loco," MacDermott answered.

MacDermott tossed another chunk of wood into the fire, showering the night with sparks, remembering the past four years bitterly.

They had split up shortly after ending the search for Thorn to escape the South Pass posse. MacDermott had hidden in the hills near Bannack City with Morris and Livingston. Lonesome Harry and Tillis weren't as lucky. The posse killed Tillis and hanged Harry from the nearest tree, but not until Harry told everything he knew about the ambush, including the murder of Alec Dunbar and disappearance of Lee Thorn. Thus the legend of the curse of Dunbar's gold had been born.

MacDermott laughed to himself at a bit of irony. Had those posse members not been so bloodthirsty, had they given Lonesome Harry a fair trial and legal execution, his testimony probably would have cleared Wesley Anderson. Instead, the only names Harry mentioned were Major Jonathan Vaughn MacDermott and Lee Thorn. So in most of the stories, it was Mac-Dermott himself who gunned down Alec Dunbar and mortally wounded Lee Thorn, when in fact Lane Morris had pulled the trigger. And Paul Livingston was free to ride about Wyoming Territory without fear, free to become a lawman and spy, while MacDermott watched his gang wither to nothing as he was forced to live like some animal in the woods.

As Lee Thorn had done for years.

"Wesley."

Anderson rose and walked slowly to the tent. He hadn't slept—nor had anyone that night—and now it was dawn, the glow of the rotting wood had finally died, and the fire no longer roared. Cora's eyes were red from lack of sleep, and she nodded sadly at Hohops.

"He's calling for you," she said.

Wes knelt beside the old man, slightly squeezing the Indian's hand. Hohops's black eyes opened, focusing first on Anderson before landing on Cora. He smiled weakly. Blood trickled from the corner of his mouth.

"Be not saddened, young lady," he said softly, grimacing with each word. "I came to this mountain to die."

He wheezed. The blood in his mouth bubbled slightly, and he turned to Anderson. Desperation filled his voice. "Mother Earth did not know all . . . did not . . . tell me . . . of . . . the bear man!" Now he yelled in agony, and Cora shut her eyes and turned away. "Joseph! Why did you leave me, Joseph?" Wes released the old man's hand. Hohops was delirious, talking to his own people. "Seeskoomkee, my old friend. I . . ."

The *tewat* mumbled something in Nez Percé. The sucking noise coming from the ugly bullet hole sickened Wesley. Hohops shuddered, and he looked up at Anderson again. His voice seemed steady, no longer racked with pain.

"Wesley Anderson," he said, "do not enter the cave. All that awaits you there is . . ." Hohops never finished the sentence. The sucking noise stopped, and the black eyes dimmed. Wes bowed his head, closed Hohops's eyes, and pulled the woolen blanket over the Nez Percé holy man's face.

Anderson led Cora to the fire, where Livingston knelt making coffee.

"The old man dead?" MacDermott asked.

Cora nodded.

"Lane," MacDermott said. "You killed him. You bury him."

Morris swore. Daylight had snapped him out of his terrified daze and returned his vicious nature. "Let him bury'm," he said, gesturing toward Anderson.

"No," MacDermott said. "Wesley and Paul have to find the horses that ran off last night. And then I've got something else planned for Mr. Anderson." He smiled slightly.

"What do you mean?" Cora asked.

"We came up here for Alec Dunbar's gold, lady. I'm betting that Lee Thorn could take us right to it. But first we got to catch my old partner."

All they found were the pack mules and two horses. As scared as those horses were, Wesley figured the rest were probably grazing in some far-off valley by now. Wes and Paul returned the livestock to the rope corral early that afternoon, and this time Anderson picketed and hobbled the animals before helping himself to a cup of coffee and the last of the bacon.

"Lee knew these mountains better than anyone, Indians included," MacDermott was telling Livingston and Morris. "He could be anywhere. Man's mind must be completely gone now; that's why he's been hiding up here for so long."

"He might not know where that gold is," Cora suggested.

"Only one way to find out," MacDermott countered.

Paul Livingston shook his head and sipped some coffee. "It's just hard to believe Thorn's still alive. He must have been killing all those prospectors and trappers who have been up here searching for the gold. So much for Dunbar's curse."

"So what now?" Morris asked.

"We track down Thorn," MacDermott said, turning to Wes. "I'm glad we didn't kill you, Anderson. You're about to earn your keep."

They left—all of them—moving on foot, following the trail Thorn had left in his flight from camp. The trail wasn't difficult. Thorn's heavy prints could easily be read in the wet ground. Anderson and Livingston scouted ahead, while MacDermott and Morris followed with Cora, her hands bound tightly with a rawhide strip.

Deeper into the woods, they began climbing a steep grade as the trees thinned out. The wind was colder up here, threatening snow, and Anderson shook despite his Mackinaw coat. He was looking at the sky, searching for a warning of snow, when he saw the cave.

Cautiously Livingston and Anderson entered the dark cavern, sweating in spite of the cold, groping around the walls. It was shallow—both men were thankful of that—and even more thankful that the cave was empty. Despite wanting to find the gold, neither man really wanted to tackle Lee Thorn. Wes Anderson, especially, felt that way. Once was more than enough for him.

Thorn's trail, however, ended at the rocks. Wes could appreciate that. The old man might be totally insane, but he hadn't lost all of his abilities. He had managed to survive for four years in the harsh high country, and knew enough to fear Anderson's Navy Colt back in camp; he still knew how to hide his tracks.

Eating jerky outside the empty cave, the outlaws rethought their plan. They couldn't spend much more time looking for Thorn before having to return to camp. In fact, now they regretted not leaving someone behind to guard the horses and supplies. Thorn could double back and steal everything, leaving them facing certain death.

"We have another option," MacDermott said, "rather than go looking for Lee."

He smiled. "We let Lee come to us—and I think I know how."

Vaughn MacDermott stared directly at Wes Anderson.

*   *   *

Wesley sat in a small clearing about a half-mile from the main camp, leaning against an uprooted tree with a small fire glowing in front of him. It was dark, cold, and creepy, silent except for the crackling fire and his own heart pounding. Slowly Anderson brought out his pennywhistle and began to play.

Lee Thorn liked music, MacDermott had said, and was often humming some ballad or ditty, out of tune in a nonmusical voice. The man was tone deaf, but that didn't stop him from trying. And he loved to listen.

It had been Anderson's pennywhistle, MacDermott had suggested, that lured Thorn into camp. So now they were staking Anderson out like bait to lure a wolf, while Livingston and MacDermott waited in the darkness. "Don't worry, partner," Livingston had said earlier, "they say music calms the savage beast." But Thorn hadn't been calm when he attacked him earlier.

Besides, Anderson was worried about Cora, alone in the main camp with Lane Morris. What if Thorn didn't take the bait here and went instead to the main camp? Or what if Lane Morris . . .

Anderson swallowed and blew a badly sounding note.

A rough version of "The Vacant Chair" began and gradually started to resemble the tune. Something cracked in the night—a dead branch maybe—and Anderson hit another wrong note, swallowed, and continued. Over the music, he heard footfalls to his left and his hands began to shake and his stomach churned.

This was much worse than playing for the warden back in prison.

At least the warden hadn't tried to kill him.

As Anderson finished ''The Vacant Chair'' and tried to think of another song, something roared in the bushes and leaped into his camp.

Anderson dropped the pennywhistle and stood quickly, as Thorn's left leg scattered the small fire and turned the camp into total darkness. The man lunged, and Anderson leaped to his right, knowing he had moved too late even before the wild man wrapped his arms around his body and lifted him with ease in a backbreaking bear hug.

Arms pinned at his side, Anderson couldn't move as he groaned for breath and help. The man was roaring like a grizzly, so loudly he couldn't hear Livingston and MacDermott, so focused on Wes that he didn't see the flaming torch or Henry rifle. Thorn suddenly stopped yelling and grunted, and Anderson heard Livingston's rifle butt smashing Thorn's head. Thorn released his grip, and Anderson dropped to his knees.

MacDermott held a torch as Livingston bashed the back of Thorn's head again, then twice, thrice more until Thorn finally fell to his side, unconscious from blows that would have killed most men.

Anderson managed to sit up. His ribs, surprisingly, weren't broken, and he searched for his pennywhistle, wiping the instrument on his pants involuntarily, and struggled to his feet.

''Well,'' MacDermott ordered, ''don't just stand there. Help Paul drag him back to camp.''

* * *

Lee Thorn sat bound, hands, feet, legs, and arms, with every piece of rope and rawhide the outlaws could find. Plus, Paul Livingston had remembered a pair of handcuffs from his saddlebags and slapped them tightly on the mountain man's wrists.

They waited, keeping a careful distance and firearms cocked, all except Cora and Anderson, left alone in Breckenridge's tent as Cora rebandaged Anderson's side; the wound had broken open during the fight with Thorn.

"Cora," Anderson said, "we're gonna have to make a move pretty soon. Our hand's about played out and MacDermott will kill us."

"I know, Wes," she said. Anderson took her right hand in his. Her skin was soft, and Anderson felt the urge to kiss her.

He was about to, when he heard MacDermott: "He's coming to."

Lee Thorn's good eye bore a hole through MacDermott, but he did not speak. His gaze turned to Livingston and Morris and as Cora and Anderson approached, he studied them, but only for a second. His intense stare at last settled on MacDermott while the other eye wandered about.

"Hello, Lee," MacDermott said. "Remember us?"

Thorn only blinked.

"Maybe he can't talk?" Livingston said.

"Wes said he shouted no when he pulled the Colt on him," Livingston offered, "He can talk."

"Maybe he doesn't like talking to trash," Cora snapped, and Anderson saw Thorn smile.

"He understands us," said MacDermott, who also saw the smile.

Morris stood suddenly and slapped Thorn savagely with a backhand. "Where is the gold, you old fool?" he exploded, but Thorn didn't budge, didn't even blink at the blow.

"Lee," MacDermott said softly, as if he were addressing a child. "I think it's time we split up that gold. We've waited for a long time. Then we can go to Bannack, maybe get you a woman, play some cards, drink some whiskey—just like old times, eh?"

Thorn remained unmoved by his former partner's speech; exasperated, Morris shouted, "This is worthless!"

Cora, however, felt sorry for the man as she stared at his battered face. Slowly she went to the campfire and filled a mug with soup, walked back to Thorn, and began spooning the broth into his mouth. "Careful," Anderson said. Thorn had killed those prospectors searching for the gold. He had almost crushed Wes to death with his bare hands.

But soon Anderson realized Cora had nothing to fear from the man. Thorn groaned in pleasure at the soup, and Cora smiled. "I bet it's been a while since you had tomato soup."

Thorn nodded.

"Lucky for us I found the can in the tent," she said. "My father liked tomato soup too."

"Yeah," MacDermott said, standing, "you eat some food and get a good night's rest and we'll talk some more in the morning.'' He and Morris disappeared into the tent. Livingston found a spot against a tree to take the first watch, and Anderson watched Cora as she fed the giant killer.

After a second helping of soup, Thorn nodded off to sleep, and Cora stood slowly. Anderson put his arm around her shoulder and escorted her to her bedroll, then drifted to his own. He was dead tired himself.

Chapter Eighteen

At breakfast, Cora fed the man moldy hardtack and bad coffee, an unappetizing meal for anyone, but Thorn didn't seem to mind. The three killers and Anderson sat by the campfire eating silently. Wes beamed as he watched Cora. He thought of her feeding her children—*their* children—patiently. *That's forward of me,* he said to himself. Realization struck him. He had fallen in love with Cora Breckenridge. Not that that had been difficult.

Anderson's smile widened as Cora wiped Thorn's mouth and asked, "All done?" Thorn nodded. Wesley's grin disappeared. MacDermott and his men approached Lee Thorn again, repeating their questions about Dunbar's gold. Anderson knew he loved Cora, knew he'd have to kill MacDermott—Morris and Livingston too—to save her life. And he understood that he'd probably die himself.

"I don't think he even knows who we are," Livingston said after an hour of fruitless questions, pleas, and threats. MacDermott sighed reluctantly and stood up. He was halfway to the coffeepot when he heard Thorn grunt.

"Major," the man said in a dry, cracking voice, "I've been waitin' for you."

And Lee Thorn laughed.

Vaughn MacDermott knelt beside Thorn, breathing excitedly, eyes bright. Morris and Livingston stood close behind him, while Anderson and Cora kept their distance. Anderson looked for a chance to escape, but the killers had all of the guns, and making a break for the woods would be too risky.

"Lee," MacDermott said, "do you know where the gold is?"

Thorn grunted. "I hid it," Thorn said, his audience listening intently. "I hid it good, then killed those that got too close. It's our gold, Major, and I've been waitin' for you to come get it."

MacDermott smiled at his good fortune. The half-wit had forgotten who it was that had ordered Morris to kill him. "Can you tell us where you hid it?"

Thorn laughed and began to hum "The Vacant Chair." He motioned with a nod at Anderson. "He plays real good, don't he?"

Nodding—MacDermott would have agreed to anything—the the outlaw leader redirected his question. "The gold, Lee, can you tell us where it is?"

"It's in my cave," Thorn said, and laughed again. "Some Injuns come up here once, but I scared them away from the cave and they don't come no more."

Livingston and Morris licked their lips. Thorn nodded. "I take you to it. Even split, right, Major?"

Jonathan Vaughn MacDermott, Connecticut native, Confederate deserter, gentleman and murderer, smiled and stood quickly. "Absolutely, Lee. It'll be just like before."

MacDermott, Livingston, and Morris gathered in a semicircle and held a brief conference. Cora knelt beside Thorn, holding a cup of coffee to his lips. Wesley sat on his haunches by the morning fire and rubbed his sweaty palms on his pants. His time was about to run out. And Cora's. If Thorn led MacDermott to the gold, they were dead.

"Anderson," MacDermott called, "come over here." Wes swallowed, glanced at Cora, and walked to the killers. *Anderson's luck?* he wondered. When he stopped, he saw a flash in Morris's right hand and felt something slam into his head.

"Noooooooooooooooo!" Thorn's scream muffled Cora's own cry, and the outlaws turned to face him as Morris cocked his revolver and prepared to kill the unconscious Texan. "Don't hurt him!" Thorn shouted. "He plays real good!"

Cora swept past the gunmen and knelt by Anderson, cradling his bleeding head. She half-expected Morris to finish them both, but the bullet never came.

"Put the gun away," MacDermott said softly. When Cora looked up, MacDermott stood smiling at the bound giant. "No need to worry, Lee. We'll just tie him up, make sure he doesn't run off before we get back with the gold.'' MacDermott frowned and led his companions toward the rope corral.

"Paul," he said, "you come with me and Thorn. Lane," and he lowered his voice, "you stay here, wait till we have been gone awhile, then kill them both."

Morris grinned; Paul Livingston swallowed.

Wes Anderson awoke with his head pounding. He leaned against a tree, his hands bound behind his back, as Cora dabbed the knot on his head with a wet bandanna. Still alive. That surprised him as he watched MacDermott and Livingston untie Thorn's feet and legs and remove some ropes across his arms. They left the handcuffs and a few other ropes on to keep the leviathan secure.

Morris sat across from them, sharpening his knife. His pistol was holstered, and Anderson's Navy Colt lay in its holster on the ground, well out of Wesley's immediate reach. He would have to untie his hands, somehow, run for the gun, and kill Morris before the killer shot him full of holes. It was suicide, he knew, but if he could just outlast the gunman, Cora might stand a chance.

Livingston stripped a mule's pack, carrying only a few ropes and a lantern, and pulled the animal behind him as MacDermott followed Thorn out of camp. Paul stopped by Morris and held out his rifle. "This might come in handy," he said, "and I'm gonna need both hands with this mule after we load her down with gold."

Morris took the Henry and leaned it against a nearby stump. "Thanks," he said, "but I got plans for this.'' He held out his knife and grinned without humor.

Livingston tugged at the revolver in his shoulder holster and reached into his pocket for some jerky. He bit off a piece, walked to Anderson, and put his right hand on his Wesley's shoulder. ''Hope to see you soon,'' he said, pressing something hard and cold against the bare skin of Anderson's neck.

Wesley's eyes met Livingston's stare. Paul smiled. ''Nine times, partner. You're all out of lives,'' he whispered, and dropped something behind Anderson's back.

Livingston turned and pulled the mule after MacDermott and Thorn.

As soon as they had disappeared, Anderson felt around behind him with his fingers, slowly to avoid alerting Lane Morris. He knew what Livingston had dropped even before his fingers found his pocketknife, the blade open.

Wes worked the rawhide against the knife eagerly, knowing he didn't have much time. It was hard work, but because Lane Morris watched him closely he couldn't have Cora just cut the cords. He would look at Morris, glance at the Navy Colt, slowing working his hands up and down against the blade.

''Cora,'' he finally said, ''go put some wood on the fire or something.'' She stood to go, but Morris motioned her down with his knife.

''Y'all lovebirds just sit there together,'' he said, ''where I can watch you better.'' He grinned. ''Then in a little bit, me and you, gal, is gonna get better acquainted.''

The rawhide snapped, and Anderson pulled free. But his case was still hopeless. A pocketknife wouldn't do any good from this distance, and he had measured his gun at five steps and a good dive away. What he needed was a diversion. But he couldn't think of one—and he wouldn't risk using Cora to help. Lane Morris would kill her without a second thought.

Finally, Morris sheathed his knife, stood up, and stretched before picking up Livingston's Henry. ''Well,'' he said, ''I reckon it's about that time.''

The metallic click of the rifle's hammer being thumbed back sounded sinister. Morris had taken three steps toward the couple when something sounded in the distance. Gunfire, just audible above the wind— but a lot of it. Morris looked back, knowing something had gone wrong.

When he turned around, Wesley Anderson dived for the Colt.

Cora screamed as Morris brought the Henry to his shoulder and drew a bead on Anderson's back. She ran toward Morris, knowing she was too late, as he pulled the trigger. The hammer snapped loudly on an empty chamber. With a savage swear, Morris tossed the Henry to the ground and reached for his holstered Remington.

Anderson hit the ground with a thud and gripped the butt of his pistol with both hands, rolling over and lifting the gun—holster and all—as he cocked it.

Cora dropped to her knees and found the barrel of the rifle. She glimpsed Wesley rolling over, saw Morris jerk his head toward her. By then she had a firm grip on the rifle and swung it like a club, striking hard against the killer's knees.

Lane Morris staggered and swore but didn't fall. He ignored the woman and jerked the Remington. The revolver was halfway drawn when Anderson pulled the trigger—shooting through the holster. The explosion was muffled as the lead ball blew out the protective closed leather bottom and sped its way into Lane Morris's chest.

The killer swayed and fired a round harmlessly into the ground. Anderson slung the holster away to get a better aim, yelling at Cora to get out of the way. He saw her drop the rifle and dive to her left. Morris still stood, clawing at the revolver, as Wes cocked and fired again. Blood spurted from Morris's stomach, and he dropped his pistol as Anderson's Colt boomed again. Another red stain appeared on Morris's shirt and widened as he fell to his knees.

Anderson thumbed back the hammer again, but held his fire. Blood began seeping out of Morris's mouth, and his eyes glazed over. He fell hard to his side, jerked once, and was still.

In the distance, the wind still carried the sounds of dying gunfire from higher up the mountain.

He moved with a purpose, reloading the Navy and strapping on his gun belt. He picked up Livingston's rifle. *Nine times,* Wesley thought. If the Henry had been loaded, Anderson and Cora would be dead now. He found some shells in the tent and loaded the rifle, stuck Morris's heavy Remington in his waistband, and headed for the picketed horses. Wes listened for more gunfire, but the faint noise had faded.

He handed Cora the rifle. ''Take a horse and get out of here,'' he said.

''No.''

''Cora,'' he said, grabbing her shoulders, ''I have to see what's happened. Don't wait. Head down the mountain. Stay to the trails and move hard and fast.''

''Wes,'' she pleaded.

''Move.''

''You'll need the rifle.''

''I'm not much good with a long gun.'' He swore then. ''Cora, get out of here!''

''Wes.'' This time there was a softness in her voice. Tears welled in her eyes. ''I won't leave you. I . . . love you.''

Anderson bent down and kissed her. ''I love you too. But I've got to find out what happened.'' He swung into the saddle. ''I'll catch up,'' he said softly.

The mule grazed at the foot of a steep ridge, picketed there because it was an impossible climb for the animal. Anderson dismounted, checked both revolvers, and started up.

An eerie silence greeted him at the top of the ridge, and Anderson followed the trail cautiously, careful not to lose his footing on the loose shale and granite. The wind was cold, but he moved on, rounded a corner, and froze.

The grizzly stopped and stood, letting out a deafening roar. Wesley measured the distance between him and the beast at twenty yards. Now he wished he had taken Livingston's rifle. Not that it would do much good against a bear, but it would pack more of a punch than two six-guns.

The white-tipped ends of the grizzly's fur bristled. Anderson had seen bears before, but this one towered over them all. It had to be nine feet tall and weigh close to a half-ton. Wes saw the blood dripping from the she-bear's snout and long, heavy claws on her forepaws. He also noticed the wounds in the grizzly's shoulder and chest. Blood seeped through the small holes, but the bullets seemed only to anger the animal.

MacDermott and Livingston had shot at the bear. That had been the source of the gunfire. But where were MacDermott, Livingston, and Thorn now? Dead? Or on the trail? Anderson quickly put those questions aside. The grizzly roared again and dropped to all fours.

Anderson knew he couldn't outrun a grizzly, but he wasn't about to just stand there and be killed. He glanced to his right as the she-bear charged.

Chapter Nineteen

Anderson leaped onto a small boulder and jumped up to the lowest branch of the small pine, which shot up near the rocky mountain face about twenty feet from a narrow, deep hole. He heard the bear's vicious roar as he pulled himself into the tree. Intense pain shot through his left ankle and he looked down to see the heel of the boot sail to the ground and blood spill from the massive tears in the leather. Wes saw anger in the grizzly's eyes as he pulled himself onto a higher limb and drew the Remington from his waist.

The .44 wouldn't kill the she-bear, but it might scare her off. The pine couldn't support the bear's massive weight, so she wouldn't climb up after him, and when the grizzly dropped on her feet, Wesley thought she might move off. Instead, the bear stood again and rammed her massive forepaws into the pine and began pushing.

Anderson swore in surprise. The revolver tumbled

171

to the earth as he grabbed limbs for support. The pine tilted. He saw the roots pull free from the wet earth, and suddenly the tree went crashing toward the ground, the roots popping, spraying the bear with mud.

Wesley screamed as he fell. The trunk of the pine smashed against the rocks as the top swayed over the edge of the deep chasm. Anderson heard the grizzly's satisfied bellow as he plummeted into the pit. The last thing he remembered was the ground racing up to meet him.

His face felt wet and cold. Slowly his eyes opened and he saw the small white flakes floating toward him, tingling his cheeks and melting instantly. Anderson sat up and leaned against the chasm's wall. The left sleeve was ripped to shreds, and he saw an ugly cut, already clotted, on his forearm and a black-and-blue bruise covering the back of his hand. A sharp pain in his back made him wince, and he ground his teeth. He tried to take off his mangled left boot but couldn't. The ankle was too swollen, the calf tender and bloody. Instead, he wrapped his bandanna tightly around the injury and looked up, shielding his eyes from the snow with his right hand.

The treetop lay still thirty feet above him. The rocky wall was slick from snow and moss. He knew he'd never be able to climb up, not without a rope, not without help. *Anderson's luck* had struck one last time. Wes leaned back and fell asleep.

"Wesley."

His eyes fluttered, and he awoke. The snow had

stopped, but the cold numbed him. At first, he thought he had been dreaming, but he heard her voice again. "Wesley."

"Cora!" Anderson shouted, pulling himself to his feet, favoring his left leg and clutching the crevice's wall with his right hand for support.

"Where are you?"

"Down here! By the tree!"

Her face appeared. Anderson's heart raced. "The mule," he said, shivering. "Get a rope from the mule's pack." She nodded and disappeared. Wes hobbled forward, clenching and unclenching his left hand. Pain shot through his fingers down to his wrist, but he'd have to use both hands to climb out of this pit. Cora returned in twenty minutes—though to Wesley it seemed like twenty hours—secured the lariat to the uprooted pine, and tossed the rope into the chasm.

Three times he slipped, once when he was only ten feet from the top, but on the fourth attempt, his right arm wrapped around the tree and he pulled himself forward. He felt Cora beside him, grunting as she gripped the waistband of his trousers and heaved. Wesley rolled over onto the rocky ground, chest ready to burst, the frigid air burning his lungs.

We waited half a minute before scrambling another twenty feet and sank into the muddy patch beside the pine's roots. He wanted to be as far away from that abyss as possible. The bear's tracks led away from the tree, westward, and Anderson prayed she didn't return. He told Cora what had happened as she rewrapped the bandanna around his ankle.

Cora had brought Livingston's rifle, and after catching his breath, Anderson stood, using the Henry as a crutch.

"Let's get out of here, Wesley," Cora said, but Anderson shook his head.

"I've got to find MacDermott and Paul," he said.

She followed him. Anderson knew better than to protest, and this time he wanted her company, needed her help. He hobbled awkwardly on the damp ground. The snow had stuck only to the higher rocks and tree limbs, but it had turned the granite and shale path slick. Anderson drew and cocked his Colt and moved cautiously, the stock of the Henry cracking against the stones, slipping on about every third step, the cold barrel pressing painfully into his left hand.

Finally, Cora took the rifle from Wesley's hand and made him lean against her. Together, they moved easier now. An hour later, both stopped and hugged the rocky wall with their backs. Anderson swallowed. He heard the deep, unearthly moaning. His breath was short, his heart pounded against his rib cage. The Lair Which Weeps lay before them, a dark, foreboding cave.

Wes looked at Cora. She couldn't hide the fear in her eyes, but she nodded, and they moved forward, stopping at the edge of the cave. "I'm all right," Wesley said, and pulled away from her, balancing himself on his good leg as he brought his revolver up and peered into the blackness inside.

He looked down and almost vomited, jerking his head back from the sight on the ground.

It was Vaughn MacDermott—or what was left of him.

"Oh my—" Cora started and gagged, sitting heavily on the ground and burying her head between her knees.

"Stay here," Wesley said. This time, Cora didn't protest.

An overturned lantern was beside the bloody mangled body of the outlaw leader. Anderson holstered his revolver, found a match, and lit the wick. At MacDermott's feet, just inside the cave, were the man's two Colts. Anderson checked the loads and saw all twelve rounds had been spent, and both barrels were stained with blood. Giant, bloody paw prints led away from the cave, and Wesley understood what had happened. By surprising the grizzly, which had entered the cave to hibernate, Vaughn MacDermott had paid a bloody price. And Livingston and Thorn?

The cave moaned—it had to be the wind, Anderson tried to assure himself as he entered, lantern in his left hand and Colt in his right. He saw more blood, glistening in the lantern's light, and found Lee Thorn.

It was obvious the man was dead. He sat against the cave's wall in a pool of his own blood, the she-bear had ripped his throat and chest, and both of his legs were broken. Anderson coughed, choked then forced himself to call out.

"Paul?" His voice sounded weak, broken. He cleared his throat and spoke Livingston's name again, louder this time, and heard a faint voice above the eerie wind.

"Partner . . ."

Anderson turned and limped to the other side of the cave, where Paul Livingston leaned against a sharp boulder. Wesley knelt beside the man who had saved his life nine times. He felt a lump in his throat as the light shone on the Mississippian. Livingston's left arm had been ripped to shreds, there were huge claw marks on his face and chest and both legs had been mauled. But somehow Livingston smiled. In his right hand, he still clutched a leather pouch, the initials A.D. burned into the grain. A gold nugget the size of a thumbnail tumbled out and bounced on the cave's floor. The pouch followed with a heavy thump.

"Ol' Lee set us up for sure," Livingston said painfully. "Led us here . . . grizzly didn't . . ." He coughed again. "Reckon you took . . . care of Lane."

Anderson said softly, "Thanks to you."

"Yeah," Livingston said. "Cora?"

"She's fine."

Livingston nodded. "Things didn't—" He coughed again. "Didn't work out . . . like I . . . planned." He nodded toward Thorn's body. "Man laughed the whole time . . . even when that grizzly . . . was killing him. Guess he . . . had been waiting . . . to kill us."

Anderson felt his entire body tremble—and it wasn't because of the cold.

"Paul, I'm gonna get you out of here."

Livingston shook his head. "Don't bother, partner . . . back's broken . . . and . . . I'm . . ." He groaned. "You get outta here . . . back to Cora. We . . . stung that grizzly . . . but she'll be back—and mad."

She was mad all right, Wes thought, but said nothing. Livingston motioned at the Navy Colt in Wesley's right hand.

"Appreciate it if you'd . . ." He closed his eyes and coughed harshly.

Anderson understood. He sat the .36 across Livingston's waist, and slowly rose. Livingston opened his eyes and smiled again. "Get going, Wes."

"Good-bye, partner," Anderson said and hobbled away, not looking back, ignoring MacDermott's body. Cora stood away from the gory entrance as Wesley limped outside. She stared at him questioningly, and sadly he shook his head. Wes leaned against her for support, and they turned away. Above the moaning of the wind came the muffled report of a pistol from inside the cave.

Wes stopped. Paul Livingston deserved better, he thought, but the wind had picked up, the sky turned gray, and Anderson lacked the strength and time to bury those men.

He turned to Cora and said, "Let's go. Far, far from here."

Her blue eyes locked on him. "You're leaving the gold?" she asked.

Anderson answered quickly, easily, honestly: "I don't want a thing to do with that gold."

Cora smiled, kissed Wesley's cheek, and helped him down the mountain.

Epilogue

December 1886

Cold weather always brought a dull ache to Anderson's left ankle, and this winter had been especially harsh. He stomped snow from his boots before entering the warmth of the Grasshopper Saloon in Bannack City. He hung his coat and wool muffler on the rack and walked, favoring his left leg just slightly, to the body wrapped in blankets on the billiard table.

One of Jack Beeler's girls stood behind the bar, winding the wall clock with a big silver key. Another girl stood behind the bar, sipping coffee. Both of them wanted nothing to do with the gaunt, dying man Beeler had found on the Virginia City road.

"He said he had been prospectin' in the mountains south of the Tetons," Beeler told Anderson. "You know how far away that is, Marshal?"

178

Anderson nodded. "That's about all I could get out of him before he went to sleep," the saloonkeeper continued. "I went through his war bag, found a book and two letters, but nothing else. I didn't read them letters, though, Marshal. Figured I'd leave those to you. Doc comin'?"

"He'll be here shortly, Jack," Anderson said, and peeled back the blankets. The man's left arm had been amputated years earlier, just below the shoulder joint, and his right hand and forearm were black from frostbite. He looked ancient. His breath was short, and Anderson doubted if the old miner would be alive by the time Doc Jessup got here.

"Let me see those things," Anderson said. Beeler handed him the war bag and remarked, "Fella must be mad to go prospectin' in them mountains in the dead of winter."

Anderson pulled the book from the canvas sack and felt his heart skip. *Yellow Gold & Red Death*, an eight-year-old Beadle and Adams Twenty Cent Novel by L. A. Chapman. He saw the subtitle: *Being a True Account of the Legend of the Curse of Alec Dunbar's Fortune*. He skimmed the opening page before pulling out the letters.

"How about a cup of coffee, Jack?" Anderson suggested.

"Want me to sweeten it with some whiskey?"

"Sure."

He just wanted Jack Beeler away from him as he opened one of the letters and read:

May 2, 1886

J. B. Brown
The American Publishing Company
Hartford, Conn.

Dear Mr. Brown:

I once thought that by writing *Yellow Gold & Red Death*, I could purge the legend of Alec Dunbar's gold from my life. After all, I lost my left arm in an accident while searching for those gold nuggets in 1877—I guess you can call me a victim of Dunbar's curse. Yet years later, I still cannot get that money from my mind.

With your permission, sir, I would like to take to those mountains once again in search of the fortune. If I am successful, I hope you would be interested in publishing my memoirs.

Sincerely,
L. A. Chapman
Antelope Hotel
Douglas, Wyoming Territory

And the reply, dated May 29:

Dear Mr. Chapman:

Received with interest your letter dated 2nd inst., and must admit we would be delighted to see your memoirs if you find Dunbar's fortune. Neither I nor our editors were familiar with the robbery and so-called curse, but your *Yellow*

Gold & Red Death fascinated and entertained us tremendously.

We wish you luck in your endeavors.

Sincerely,
J. B. Brown
The American Publishing Company

"Anderson!"

The rattling voice startled Wes as he lowered the letters and stared into the old man's hollow eyes. Anderson subconsciously bit his lower lip and felt a shiver run up his backbone. Since leaving Wyoming Territory in the fall of '77, he had been using the name William Anderson. He let Wesley Anderson, convict and robber, remain drowned in the Laramie River. At first, Wes thought this old-timer might be someone he had served with in the "Big House," but finally he recognized the haggard face.

Anderson's lips parted. "Louie Chapman," he said softly. The bartender from South Pass City, the man who had ambushed Wesley and Paul Livingston at Cora's cabin, the man whose life Anderson had spared. Suddenly, it all made sense.

Chapman mouthed something, but Anderson couldn't hear, so he bent over the man until his ear was just above the old bartender's mouth. Yet he still strained to understand the broken, dry voice.

"I found the gold," Chapman said.

Anderson swallowed.

"Bones. The bones of men. In a cave."

"Here's your coffee, Marshal," Beeler's voice sounded behind him.

"Shut up, Jack," Anderson snapped.

Chapman fought for breath, blinked once, and said, "Gold. In the Lair Which Weeps. It moaned, too, Anderson. But . . . it . . . it . . . also . . ." The old man coughed roughly, licked his lips and continued:

"I heard laughter. Men screaming. A bear roaring. Gunshots."

Wes straightened, unbelieving, staring into Louie Chapman's eyes. He recalled the line he had just read in Chapman's book—*A reasonable man could attribute the wail inside the mountain to the wind, but even the most hardened cynic would be hard-pressed to explain the mocking laughter*. But that had been written, Wes knew, about Lee Thorn, when he hid in the cave and scared Indians, murdered prospectors . . . before Wesley had seen the old outlaw's body ripped apart by a grizzly. The only people, living, who knew about the bear and what had happened nine years earlier in that cave were Anderson and Cora—and they never spoke of it. How could Chapman have heard gunshots, a bear . . . was there really a curse?

Chapman's Adam's apple bobbed. "I left the gold," he said weakly. "Blew up the entrance. No one will . . ."

His eyes glazed over. Chapman's breathing ceased.

Two minutes passed before Anderson could move. He reached out and pulled a blanket over the dead man's face.

Jack Beeler handed Wes the cup, and he drank some.

"What was that old fella talkin' about, Marshal?" Beeler asked. "What gold?

Anderson placed the cup of coffee on a table and walked to the stove. "Nothing," he said, tossing the letters and book into the hot fire.

"Sorry for your trouble, Jack," Wesley said. "You did all you could for him. Have Doc send me a bill for the old man's burial."

Anderson pulled on his coat, wrapped the muffler around his neck, reached for the doorknob, and sighed. At first, he thought about himself, how the body of the broken, obsessed man on the billiard table could have been his own had it not been for Cora Breckenridge. And then he felt relief.

Louie Chapman said he had blown up the entrance to the Lair Which Weeps, burying Paul Livingston, Lee Thorn, and Vaughn MacDermott at last, sealing the curse of Alec Dunbar's gold forever.

"You all right, Marshal?" Jack Beeler asked.

"Yeah," Anderson said as he pulled open the door, feeling the blast of cold air. "I'm going home."